# Free
# Dakota

# Free
# Dakota

## William Irwin

Winchester, UK
Washington, USA

First published by Roundfire Books, 2016
Roundfire Books is an imprint of John Hunt Publishing Ltd., Laurel House, Station Approach,
Alresford, Hants, SO24 9JH, UK
office1@jhpbooks.net
www.johnhuntpublishing.com
www.roundfire-books.com

For distributor details and how to order please visit the 'Ordering' section on our website.

ISBN: 978 1 78535 326 0
Library of Congress Control Number: 2015956011

A CIP catalogue record for this book is available from the British Library.

This book is a work of fiction. The characters, incidents, and dialogue are the products of the
author's imagination or are used fictitiously. Any resemblance to persons, living or dead, is
purely coincidental.

Design: Stuart Davies

Printed in the USA by Edwards Brothers Malloy

We operate a distinctive and ethical publishing philosophy in all
areas of our business, from our global network of authors to
production and worldwide distribution.

# 1

As Don spent more and more weekends in Vermont, his daughter Deborah grew concerned. On the phone she asked him, "So, Dad, tell me the truth. Do you have a girlfriend?"

Don paused for a moment before answering. He had actually become monogamous with a prostitute named Casey, but he couldn't afford the relationship much longer. "No," he said, "it's politics."

"Politics!" Deborah replied. "You never cared about politics. Remember the 2000 election? I was racked with guilt for supporting Ralph Nader and costing Al Gore the election. You didn't listen to a word I said. You didn't even care about the legal aspect when the case went to the Supreme Court."

"This is different," he said.

"Different how?"

"It's not about elections or politicians."

"What's it about?"

"Freedom, I guess. I've been blogging about..."

"You've been blogging? When are you going to write another novel? It's been a year since you've made an alimony payment, and Mom is ready to take you to court."

* * *

It all started back in March. Walking into the 7-11 with his monstrous travel mug, Don went straight to the soda fountain and filled up with Coke, grabbing some Twinkies on the way to the counter.

"Sir, I can't sell you that," the cashier said.

"What?" Don asked.

"The soda, sir. There are no more Big Gulps."

"That's OK. That's why I brought my own mug."

"I still can't sell it to you, sir. It's illegal to sell a 64-ounce soda."

"So just charge me for two 32-ounce sodas."

"I can't do that, sir. Not if you're using that container."

"How about four 16-ounce sodas?"

"I can't do that either, sir. If you'd like, you can pour the soda into four 16-ounce containers. Then I can ring them up."

"No. I did that yesterday. That's why I brought my mug today."

"I'm sorry, sir."

"Come on, buddy, move it along," said the old man with the newspaper and coffee in line behind Don.

Don poured the soda on the counter, walked straight out of the 7-11, and got into his red '68 Camaro. Short distances made big differences in the landscape as you drove north in the early spring. By the time he reached the Taconic, the trees were still barren and the grass was more brown than green. He hoped to see some white by the time he reached Vermont.

Don didn't like to ski, but he had spent some lost college weekends in Killington. This winter had been mild and the snows hadn't fallen much on the Green Mountains. So his trip found little activity in Killington, just an odd political demonstration. The Second Vermont Republic. Morons clad in hemp. They wanted to secede from the Union, start their own country. As their speeches informed him, Vermont had never been an English colony, and it had actually been its own republic from 1776 until 1791. Now it was time for the Second Vermont Republic.

Walking by The Pickle Barrel, a bar where he had once puked in the bathroom, Don bumped into a knit-cap activist. "Watch where you're going, man."

"Sorry," Don said. "I wasn't paying attention."

"Well ya gotta pay attention, man. That's the problem. Big business and big government are killing us. Small and local, that's the answer. Everything I'm wearing was made in Vermont.

Everything I eat, drink, and smoke comes from Vermont."

"Sorry, I just meant I wasn't paying attention where I was walking."

"Yeah, I know what you meant, man. You're too busy drinking that big corporate soda. Here, read this."

Don took a pamphlet and returned to his car, leaving his seat belt unbuckled.

\* \* \*

*I don't know why I try,* Don thought. *I pretend to relax. I pretend it doesn't matter, but it just won't come. I mean it comes sometimes, sure, but there's no satisfaction, no sense of finality. Just some craggy pebbles at the bottom of the bowl. Nothing to wipe, but I do it anyway out of decorum. Or is it hope? Either way it's just wasted paper.*

*That's the thing about chronic constipation. You'd be willing to endure days of feeling backed up if there were some great release at the end, but no. There is just the occasional paltry product.*

"*Big Gulps are the new tattoos,*" Don blogged. "*Poor people are too stupid to be trusted to decide for themselves.*" Until 1997 New York had been one of the few places in the country where you couldn't get a tattoo. When the law was enacted in 1961 tattooing was strictly limited to the lower classes. There was no danger of middle-class kids coming home with visible marks that would kill future job opportunities. Now, though, tattooing was safe and hygienic. "*You have a greater chance of getting an infection at the doctor's office than you do at the tattoo parlor,*" Don wrote. It wasn't the new safety measures, but the new financial interests that changed the law in 1997. The city was losing lots in business and tax revenue because residents had to leave the five boroughs to get inked.

"*It's not enough to tell people that a 64-oz soda has a million calories. They're too stupid to take the hint. We have to ban the sodas. Never mind that it's still legal to buy four 16-oz sodas.*"

Don went on to imagine that a black market in 64-oz sodas would emerge and that it would become the sugar-fix equivalent of tainted heroin and back-alley abortions. *"The only solution is to keep gluttony and stupidity safe and legal."* he concluded.

In the comments section, Maxine from New Haven wrote, "In order to preserve freedom, the government has to limit freedom. When people are allowed to choose and do whatever they want, they end up making bad choices that close off the possibility of other future free choices. So the solution is to maximize their overall freedom by limiting freedom of choice in specific situations."

Lance Tucker wrote, "You can live free or die in Vermont. The government will have to take the soda from your cold dead hand, and the government of the Second Vermont Republic will not try."

When Don posted his next piece on seat belts Lance was hooked. The government has *"no right to tell me that I can't drive without a seat belt while drinking a 64-oz soda."* Don had gotten a speeding ticket, and the officer slapped on a seat-belt ticket as well. *"They had seat belts in cars in the 70s, but no self-respecting teenager would wear them. Seat belts were for old ladies and children. It was a sign of uncertainty to wear a seat belt, an admission that you might crash, an admission that you were not all powerful,"* Don wrote. Even the driving instructor eschewed the seat belt. *"He'd wear it while giving lessons, but you'd see him drive up without it."* So, in conformist mode, Don hadn't worn a seat belt in high school, and the force of habit carried Don through adulthood when he bought the car he had always wanted as a kid, a red '68 Camaro. *"Putting on a seat belt felt like putting on a big orange life preserver—an advertisement of vulnerability."* Don knew this was all nonsense. He was an adult, and he knew the dangers he exposed himself to in not wearing a seat belt. After all, *"even the world's greatest driver is still at the mercy of idiots on the road."* It was just a habit he couldn't seem to break. So maybe the ticket would help him break the habit. Maybe he should be grateful for the ticket.

"You've been screwed," wrote Lance. "You just want to make your own decisions without government interference. And they make you look like you're some kind of anarchist."

"Thanks," Don replied. "It was a wakeup call, that speeding ticket. It made things very personal. I guess it was like the sense of violation that you feel when your house is robbed. It's not so much the stuff that's been taken. It's the sense of security that's been lost. I knew I was speeding. I didn't like the feeling of being pulled over by the cop. I was able to work through the adrenaline and follow protocol, producing my license and registration. But when the officer told me that he would also be citing me for failure to wear a seat belt, he might as well have taken his billy club to my tail light and said he was fining me for the broken turn signal."

"Yeah, you were screwed. You were treated like a dangerous criminal. Meanwhile you were just John Q. Public trying to get home."

"Yeah, I guess I was."

# 2

The phone rang as Lorna watered the seeds in her windowsill garden.

"Hello, Mr. Yakimoto. We're looking forward to your visit to New York. What can I do for you?"

"I do not wish to see Ms. Amber," he said.

"I understand, Mr. Yakimoto. Kamala has arranged for Angelica to meet you in the lobby of your hotel at eight o'clock."

"Very good."

"Please let me know if there is anything else I can do to make your visit more enjoyable."

"I will," he said, and hung up.

Lorna pulled her natural blonde hair back in a ponytail, sat on her couch, and checked e-mail. Clicking a link from Kamala, she read about the Second Vermont Republic in the comments section of the *Soda Blog*. Lorna had no interest in marijuana and secession. Drugs hurt her business, and she stayed away from politics. Vermont might as well have been Greenland as far as she was concerned. Her clients didn't go there. They went to Vale, Aspen, and other more exclusive ski spots out West.

The SVR said that the little guy was held hostage to the interests of giant banks and corporations that ran the show and were considered too big to fail. If you're too big to fail and not smart enough to succeed, then that means you'll get special treatment at the cost of the little guy. "Share and share alike" would be the guiding motto of Vermont after secession. Lorna didn't like it.

* * *

After constant nudging from Lance and others, Don took up the drug issue on the *Soda Blog*, as it was now called. *"The war on drugs is a failure,*" Don declared. Citing statistics and relating anecdotes, Don made the standard case that the federal government is making no progress. Well-intentioned as Prohibition was, it did not stop the flow of alcohol. Where there is demand, supply will find a way to meet it. As with booze, so with drugs. Don stopped short of calling for legalization across the board. Some drugs seemed just too dangerous, heroin for one. But marijuana ought to be legal. He wasn't advocating the use of marijuana; he was calling for its legalization. Not only would it be safer and better; not only would it allow adults to indulge in a harmless high; not only would it reduce crime; but it would be an economic boon. *"Just the thing to jumpstart the economy."* The only conceivable objection was moralistic. But more than half the population, including three recent presidents, had smoked marijuana at some point. So the evil-and-unnatural argument was losing force. The discussion posts came from legalization advocates all over the country, most notably the SVR.

Don did not have a home. He had two-bedroom apartment on the Upper East Side that smelled of emptiness and sounded hollow. His daughter Deborah made a point of calling him regularly and inviting him to visit her family in Hastings, but that felt like the charity that it was—much appreciated and even necessary, but charity nonetheless. So, Don skipped the next weekend in Hastings and drove to Vermont.

\* \* \*

"The envelope feels a little light, Lorna," said Captain Ryan.

"I assure you, it's all there," she said.

"We agreed to an increase."

"It's in there."

Ryan sneered and put the envelope in his trench-coat pocket. He took a sip of his coffee, and slid out from the booth at the

Lexington Diner.

"See you next month, Lorna."

She nodded and looked to her phone. Kamala had sent a link to the *Soda Blog* piece on the legalization of marijuana. *Why doesn't this guy write about the legalization of prostitution?* she thought. Of course she knew why he didn't. Don Jenkins could write for the legalization of weed without being a biased advocate for his own vice—he could say, "I don't smoke marijuana and I don't encourage its use, but it should be legal." Prostitution would be different. Most of the same arguments could be made, but he would either have to admit that he was a john or be vulnerable to that discovery.

There were lots of Lance Tuckers out there advocating for the legalization of marijuana. The rhetorical question—"Have you no shame?"—was never posed because clearly they had no shame. There was still plenty of shame in the sex trade, though, both on the side of the prostitutes and the side of the johns. People openly acknowledged that they smoked marijuana. It was even chic to say you worked your way through college selling pot, but try saying that you worked your way through college selling your body. Maybe in some circles you could get away with having been a stripper. But a prostitute? No way. It still had the stain of shame. So it wasn't just a legal issue; it was a public-relations issue. As long as the shame remained, so would the law.

\* \* \*

Federal Agent Webster Daniels began his investigation of the Second Vermont Republic with simple instructions: just gather information. Of course, Rohmer and the guys in Washington didn't think there was any chance that Vermont would actually secede. They were just concerned with the kind of people who would be involved in such a movement. It might be a bunch of misguided granola-munching hippies, but it might be something more.

Daniels's southern accent had faded through the years, but it was still perceptible, especially to Northern ears. Most Vermonters did not support the SVR, but they were still not inclined to speak ill of the SVR to a Georgia cracker. People have a right to think, say, and do as they please as long as they're not harming anyone else. That seemed to be the attitude of the Vermonters who Daniels talked to, even if he suspected that many of them thought the SVR folks were kooky at best, an embarrassment at worst. No one regarded them as dangerous. There was talk of a militia, but there was no active military wing of the movement. They did not plan to secede through force. The plan was to win over the people and vote for secession. Whenever America intervened in a foreign country and whenever government money funded a crony company, the SVR would grow more vocal and organize public protests. And people would think, you know, they have a point.

Don was unimpressed by his visit to the Champlain Valley, despite its rustic charm. Most people on the commune were clueless about the SVR. Vermont as a whole didn't matter to them as much as the commune, which had been going strong for over thirty years. Lots of faces had come and gone, but there was a definite sense of continuity. And there was progress. Things were a lot easier and more comfortable than they were just five years ago. Some, like Linda, were suspicious and even resentful of Lance's entrepreneurial activity. But they pulled up short of condemning him because he was a benevolent outlaw. If he had been profiting that heavily with a legal commodity, like maple syrup, they would have excoriated him.

Lance's agitation for legalization did not sit well. Linda, of course, thought that marijuana should be legalized, but she feared what would happen if it were. The commune's production was limited by the need to avoid tripping the wires of detection. But if weed were legal, outside money and influence would make the operation so big and so crassly commercially capitalistic as to be unrecognizable.

Despite the mounting tensions, Lance retained affection for the commune and most of the Birkenstock-wearing communeists, including Linda. Still, he would have liked a pat on the back or an "atta boy" once in a while, or, God forbid, a "thank you." Instead, Linda threw her vast weight around, elbowing Lance out of her way in the kitchen, and scowling beneath her monobrow.

There were torn posters on the walls, dirty dishes in the sink, and big bongs in every room. Don had tried marijuana at parties a couple of times in the '80s, not so much out of curiosity as out of a need to conform to the rebellious pose struck by his colleagues at the law firm who threw the parties and supplied the weed. It didn't do much for him then, but it did this time. Things slowed down and the conch shell on the mantle fascinated him. Lance and Linda and the others seemed funny and wise. He could finally see what all the fuss was about. So, while Don's visit began by looking for the exit, it ended by looking for a return invitation.

Return he did many times over the next six months. That's what intrigued Agent Daniels and got him the okay from Rohmer to extend his stay in Vermont. What was this writer from New York doing with these whackos? Sure, there was public record of the first connection through the *Soda Blog*, and there was a bond formed over marijuana and legalization. But Daniels sensed more.

Don began to feel the tensions in the commune during his visits. Lance was doing more and more and less and less, and some people didn't appreciate it. Officially, the commune had no leaders, but unofficially Lance had assumed authority, and he had several guys working for him fulltime. The profits made the place run and grow, subsidizing the activities and causes of others. Lance wanted to get into direct sales because he lost a piece of the action in the final transaction. But when he raised the issue at dinner Linda spit out her tofu.

"What good could it do?" Linda asked. Chatter at the table ceased.

"Good?" Lance replied.

"Yeah, good," Linda shouted, putting her elbows on the table. "We already have everything we need. Food, water, shelter, and smoke. And for now we're not on anyone's radar. If you expand further it won't give us anything we don't already have, and the whole thing may come crashing down on us. You're already drawing too much attention with that fuckin' BMW!" Linda lit a cigarette and exhaled in exasperation.

"The business has to grow. In the long run there will be more money for everyone. And the car isn't mine, it's ours."

"Well, it's funny how no one but *you* drives *our* car. And I don't remember being consulted about what kind of car *we* should buy. I'm pretty sure *I* would have preferred a Subaru."

"The car serves a purpose, Linda. We can't move among the players in a Subaru."

"Yeah, but we can warm the planet in a BMW."

"All right. Remember it's 'From each according to his ability, to each according to his need.' I happen to need that car in order to best serve the commune according to my ability."

"If you say so, man." Linda stamped out her cigarette and left the table.

Election season provided an opportunity for the SVR to spread its message, but despite 95% statewide name recognition, the SVR couldn't get enough signatures to put a referendum for secession on the ballot. Of course they knew that there wasn't enough support for secession to win the referendum, but a ballot initiative would get national attention and set the stage for a future referendum that could succeed.

The forces that gathered under the banner of the SVR were varied. They all resented foreign wars and crony capitalism, but agreement ended there. Most in the SVR favored a vaguely socialist state in which central planning of the economy and many parts of society would be workable because the scale would be small. But Lance was developing sympathy for the libertarian wing of the SVR, led by Andy Johnson, who wanted government out of the lives of the people as much as possible. The government wouldn't centrally plan anything. People would be free to plan and succeed or fail on their own.

Law-school professors taught that law and politics were inseparable, but Don had never been a political person. In fact, he never had much interest in the law either. It had been a job for him, not a calling. Don was intrigued, though, when Lance lit another joint and engaged him with the question, "What laws would you establish if you could build a society from the ground up?"

"I don't know," Don said. "Some people need to be taken care of, but nobody likes to be forced to take care of another. That's where the 'too big' complaint makes sense. When society is too big, people don't know one another and don't feel connected to one another and don't feel inclined or obliged to help one another."

"That's right," Lance said, as he passed the joint. "Think of the Amish. They don't accept government aid when they're sick or down on their luck. They help one another."

"Yeah, it's like..." Don inhaled deeply, "as long as people get their assistance from the government..." he exhaled, "they lose sight of where the assistance really comes from...their friends and neighbors. They feel like they're entitled to it."

"It's worse than that," Lance said, taking the joint. "They resent you, man." He inhaled and continued, "The more you give them, the more they think you're taking from them." He exhaled, and the cloud of smoke lingered in Don's face.

"You're right. My ex-wife is like that. Always thinks I owe her something more."

# 3

She toppled off him with a moan. Don held her tight from behind for a moment before she rolled out of bed and began to dress in the morning light. Overflowing in all parts feminine, Casey was not typical of the girls in Lorna's catalog, but she was exactly what Don wanted. With a flick of her head Casey tamed her raven mane and bent over to kiss Don. He shuddered with a sense of alarm.

"What's the matter?" she asked.

"Nothin', Case. Just got a chill or something."

"Well, pull up the covers. I'll see you later."

"Tonight?"

She nodded and walked away, all boots and ass.

Don pulled up the covers and fell back to sleep.

It had been six months and he wasn't sure what her real story was. The only thing he knew for sure was that her real name was Casey. Don chose Casey because she was his physical type, and he kept coming back because she liked being in charge. He told her everything about himself, and she told him true lies in exchange.

Casey did not return that evening. When Don called he discovered that her phone number had been disconnected. The pain was physical. Don's whole body ached like he had the flu. He took aspirin, got into bed, and tried to read.

After a restless night, Don met Lorna at Elite Encounters in Manhattan. The office was small and sleek, black leather couches and a minimalist desk in reception leading to Lorna's suite with its view of the skyline.

"I love Casey, but I don't know what happened to her, Don," Lorna said.

"Is she okay?" Don asked. "Did someone want to hurt her?"

"She's gone. Her phone number is disconnected, and her roommate says she's moved out."

"I see," he said. Somehow Don knew Casey was going when she kissed him goodbye the previous morning. "Does this happen a lot?"

Lorna looked out the window. Wherever Casey had gone it was beyond the skyline.

"No. Most girls have an exit strategy, but few ever use it." Lorna turned to face Don. "Please be happy for Casey. Wherever she is, she's doing what she wants."

Don winced and shook his head. "What about me?"

Lorna arched an eyebrow.

"What about you, Don? I'm sorry to have to bring this up, but your credit card has been rejected."

"Well, I guess Casey won't be collecting anyway."

"Maybe not, Don. But what about me?"

"Let me take you out to dinner, Lorna."

She smirked.

"What are you going to pay with?"

"You can pay."

Lorna was not looking to replace Kent, her beau of the past two years, an investment banker she had met through mutual friends. But Don didn't talk the way everyone else did. He listened and asked questions, not just flattering questions, but the right questions, questions that took Lorna places she didn't realize she wanted to go, questions like "So, what's *your* exit strategy?"

Don had grown gray in a way that he hadn't anticipated. It suited him. He had not been at ease as a young man, but at fifty-five he had outlasted the competition who had run too hard too early. What Don got from Lorna was a mystery to her. She thrilled him in bed, but at thirty-five Lorna was not the fresh young flesh that Don had been accustomed to with Casey. Lorna had thought Don sappy and sentimental for getting so attached to Casey, but that side of him became appealing.

Lorna's future was hopelessly vague. In fact, she didn't really want to have one. She talked about chalking it all up in a few years and retiring to California, but that wasn't something she actually looked forward to or planned. The business gave her a buzz, and though she talked about expanding, the truth is that she had nowhere to expand. Lorna could cultivate new clients and keep secrets and perhaps become notorious for the celebrity crowd, but that didn't appeal to her. She needed to nurture something more substantial. Don validated those feelings and that sense of aimlessness. He didn't offer Lorna alternatives and he didn't suggest that she'd feel differently tomorrow.

\* \* \*

Lance was looking at the past through the prism of the present. He had conveniently forgotten what a cynical moocher he had been. Not the best-looking or most charming guy at Middlebury, Lance had a hard time getting action even in the free-love '70s. So in the second semester of his sophomore year, he signed up for a women's studies course and put the odds in his favor. Lance was one of three guys in a class of thirty. Some of the women resented his presence at first, but he learned the lingo and made his comments in class strategically. He would wait for a woman to make a political point, affirm what she said and take it one step further: "Not only should women get equal pay, they should get greater pay in the form of reparations for past misdeeds." He believed none of it, but he said it with conviction. And it worked. Joanne invited Lance to join the commune, and he never once paid for sex, not even in the way most guys do, with gifts, and promises, and commitments. As long as he was willing to let go of a girl and share her with another guy, there was always more for him. The miracle of the fishes and the loaves. It all just multiplied.

The near past was vivid. Lance could remember clearly that yesterday he woke early, had breakfast, read the paper, and talked on the phone for an hour before going to the greenhouses and then meeting with Andy Johnson. But when he thought about thirty years ago it was just a fog. So instead of appreciating the soil in which he took root, Lance resented it. He continued to talk the talk of "keep it small" and "stick it to the man." But the cognitive dissonance was ringing in his brain.

Morale was low for the SVR after they failed to get their referendum on the ballot. That's when the internal squabbles began. The messaging was too vague, and the reason it was too vague was that "we're too vague." That's what Brian Downing said. The SVR was a big tent that hosted malcontents of various stripes who favored the ultimate move of secession. To accommodate all those views and personalities, the slogans and press releases had been indeterminate. It was time to get specific. What did they stand for?

As leader of the socialist wing of the SVR, Downing focused their message, "Vermont for Vermont." The state's sons and daughters would no longer fight and die in foreign wars. By law, there would be no large corporations. All business would be small and local. There would be no poverty or unemployment. Businesses would pay a minimum living wage of twenty dollars an hour, and Vermonters who did not find employment in the private sector would be employed by the state. Wealth would be redistributed via taxes in accord with Rawlsian principles such that any inequality in wealth would benefit the least well off. Doctors could still be paid more than bus drivers but only as much more as was needed to attract qualified people into the medical profession. The costs of medical care would be set by the state of Vermont, which would provide insurance for all of its citizens. In addition, the price of all consumer goods would be set by the state, and imported goods would be restricted with the "buy Vermont first" policy. Marijuana would be legal, but other drugs would be prohibited. Gambling in state-run casinos would be legal. Carbon consumption would be discouraged by a carbon tax. Meat-eating would be discouraged through warning labels and high prices.

During a speech to a small crowd in a high-school gym in Burlington, Downing amped up the anti-corporate rhetoric: "Mitt Romney was right. Corporations are people. But he forgot to tell us what kind of people they are. They're psychopaths. Do you know what a psychopath is? It's a person who is unable to feel empathy, who has no emotional reaction to the pain and suffering of others. So why are corporations psychopaths? Because they feel no empathy for the people they hurt and the environmental damage they cause. They can't feel empathy because no single individual is responsible for their actions; the responsibility is diffused. Stockholders care only about the price of the stock. They're not emotionally invested in the company and not ethically invested in seeing the company do the right thing. And corporate executives care only about quarterly reports and stock prices. Their only obligation is to make money for their investors. While the buck should stop with the CEO, it rarely does. All credit flows upward but all blame flows downward. The CEO may make big decisions, but he counts on his team of executives. So he always has plausible deniability. Well, there will be no more plausible deniability in Vermont. Our people and our environment have suffered enough."

Downing's speech was recorded and posted to the SVR website where thousands watched and commented.

The small libertarian wing of the SVR was not pleased with Downing's message and rhetoric. Andy Johnson and others had hoped to work within the SVR to realize their vision, but they had been naive. All they shared in common with the rest of the SVR was disdain for the current system and its power brokers. It's not always true that the enemy of your enemy is your friend. It's true that he can be your ally, but all alliances are temporary by their nature. When terms and concerns shift, alliances crumble. So Johnson and the libertarians split off under the banner of the Free Vermont party.

Downing didn't shed a tear. Now he could distill and focus the anti-corporate message. Only a small percentage of Vermonters worked for publicly-traded corporations, so very few people saw their livelihood threatened by the rhetoric. On the other hand, all Vermonters, like all Americans, had been harmed by corporate greed. So it was a message that resonated. It made sense of what had happened with the economic downturn and it pointed the finger at unlikeable people, those bastards from Wall Street who had pissed on Main Street.

"Smaller is better," Downing said to a large gathering in a high-school gym in Montpelier. "Small towns are safer and friendlier than big cities. Small means people looking out for one another and caring for one another." The microphone crackled with feedback. "The United States of America has the same big-scale problems that corporations have. Think of the moral hazard of the president and Congress sending people to die in wars they have started." A piercing sound whistled through the microphone. Downing left his notes and the microphone behind. Stepping in front of the podium, he began to shout, "The sons and daughters of Congress don't die in the deserts and jungles of foreign lands, because they don't join the military. Only the sons and daughters of the poor lose limbs in uniform. For them, it's the best option—better than flipping burgers. When the politicians make the call and gather the glory while the people pay in blood, the system cannot be sustained. Smaller means no perpetual cycle of war. It means peace and prosperity."

Downing was confident that, with its focused message, the SVR could gain the necessary support to put a referendum on secession on the ballot in two years. The following summer, though, Andy Johnson began a campaign for state senate under the banner of the Free Vermont party. The rift between the SVR and Free Vermont didn't split many families or friendships, but it did cause problems on the commune when Lance put a "Johnson for State Senate" bumper sticker on the BMW.

Pointing to the car, Linda said, "So now you're a Republican?"

"What are you talking about?" Lance replied.

"The bumper sticker—Johnson?"

Lance grimaced.

"He's not a Republican, Linda. You know that. He was part of the SVR and now he's split off to form a new party—Free Vermont."

"Doesn't sound so free to me. Sounds like he favors corporations and big business and all the evil things the SVR opposes."

Lance folded his arms.

"Listen, Linda, you know he favors drug legalization and he's a strong advocate for civil liberties."

Linda got up on her toes and looked down at him, saying, "I don't care. Get *that* bumper sticker off *our* car."

Downing and Johnson had agreed that the United States of America was illegitimate and that Vermont had to become its own nation. You couldn't validate the system by running for office. But now Johnson was doing it. He was running, and he was getting lots of publicity. Downing felt his fist clenching as he read about it in the *Burlington Free Press*. To all the people who only half paid attention it probably seemed that Johnson was the SVR in a new form. He was the leader of the cause. Downing threw down the paper and took his beagle for a walk in the woods.

Andy Johnson had a powerful grip for a little guy. Was he just showing off or was this the way he always shook hands? Either way, Don was impressed as he sat down across the table at the Towne Tavern.

"I loved your line in the paper about the Occupy movement,"

Don said.

Andy squinted as if he couldn't recall, and let Crosby, Stills, and Nash fill the silence with the reminder that by the time they got to Woodstock they were half a million strong.

Don quoted him, "Their hearts are in the right place, but their feet are in the wrong place."

Andy ran his hand through his red hair. "Oh yeah. Bad sense of geography. They should have been occupying Washington, not Wall Street."

"But there was plenty of bad behavior on Wall Street."

"Sure," Andy said, "but you can't blame banks and corporations for seeking favorable treatment."

"Who do you blame, then?"

"I blame the government for giving it to them. Sometimes the too-big boys have to fail even if that means pain for all of us in the short run."

* * *

Don was spending nearly all his weekends in Vermont. He even got Lorna to join him once. Linda's eyes grew wide when Lorna appeared in the common room. Linda extended her hand in greeting, but then had to make sure she kept it from touching Lorna's blonde hair and grazing her exposed shoulder.

"It's a pleasure to meet you, Lorna," Linda said.

"The pleasure is mine, Linda," Lorna said. "Don's told me so much about you."

"Don't believe a word of it!"

"No, no, I assure you it's all good. He told me how talented you are in keeping the commune organized. Every organization needs a leader."

"Well, I'm not really a leader, just a trusted servant."

"You're too modest."

Linda blushed.

The body odor and mildew cemented Lorna's decision not to stay there. Instead, she and Don compromised, playing tourist and staying at a little B&B called the Woodhouse Country Inn just outside Middlebury. Lorna would have preferred a big hotel. Why would strangers want to sit around a breakfast table together? In this case, apparently the answer was to discuss the leaves. After breakfast, driving beneath a canopy of fall splendor, Lorna ranted, "It's not as if these people came from Arizona or California. They came from New York and Massachusetts. Weren't the leaves changing there too? Is Vermont's foliage so much better?" Lorna understood that some people were connoisseurs of fine wine and others of exotic women, but leaves seemed an odd obsession. Changing leaves were decaying organic matter, a sure sign of the gray winter to come.

Combined with this inexplicable love of dying leaves was the perverse love of old furniture. New she got. New shoes, new cars, the newest phone and computer. But why were these people so obsessed with old stuff? Sure, some of it could be neat, but most of it was junk. Vermont catered to these "leaf peepers" who wanted to take home a story of how they found this loom or that water pitcher in the quaintest little antique shop that they stumbled upon while driving through covered bridges some October weekend during "peak foliage."

Lorna concluded that it was all captured in the smell and taste of real Vermont maple syrup, a commodity too precious for the locals to use themselves. At nearly $20 for a pint, it's a perfectly extravagant reminder of the time in Vermont. The only problem, Lorna discovered, is that once you open the bottle you have to refrigerate it. No preservatives. Most people, like Lorna, don't realize this, and so they get something disgusting when they return for their second trip down maple memory lane a few weeks after the first. Others who have learned from making this mistake once find that all the charm is gone when they've refrigerated and microwaved the taste of Vermont.

Don thought that Lorna would appreciate all of this from a business perspective, but she did not. Lorna's business was "the world's oldest profession for a reason," she explained. "It's an honest exchange, money for sex." All the insincerity of the courtship dance was gone, stripped down to its basics. Of course the arrangement could be abused, and people could be taken advantage of. That was the norm for the scummy street pimps who preyed upon runaways, got them hooked on heroin, and turned them out against their will. That was not Lorna's game, though, and she felt no kinship to it. Her girls commanded top dollar because she was able to arrange their liaisons with men who could pay the premium.

Everyone got what they paid for, and everyone got the price they demanded. It was simple, but so many other people took short cuts that it was not difficult to beat the competition. In the early days, Lorna charmed girls into joining her, but she had ceased recruiting long ago. Working for Lorna had become like posing for *Playboy*, an honor. The business was her baby, but she ran it with an efficiency that might suggest she had forgotten what she was trading in. Truly, she never did.

Antique dealers and B&B operators could be cynical in seeing their customers as suckers to be fleeced. But Lorna did not, could not, see her girls and clients that way precisely because that was the way everyone else saw them. Don appreciated that, but he still raised the question, "Don't you want out of the business?"

Most people do. They want out of the business, not prostitution, but whatever business they're in. Don wanted out of lawyer-ing and then he wanted out of novel-ing—at least that's what he told himself when he was unable to write. The business becomes mundane, no matter how exciting or promising it may once have been. People want out. The grass is always greener; the foliage is always peaker. Most people have a fantasy of what they would do. Don was one of the few who succeed in living the fantasy. For every person who dreams of becoming a successful novelist and quitting his day job there are thousands who don't succeed. For most people, their fantasy is not as far-fetched as becoming a successful novelist. They just want to restore old cars, or teach underprivileged children, or open a cupcake bakery, yet they don't do it. Don't make the moves. Don't succeed. Don wasn't most people, and Don wasn't done yet.

# 4

Don rarely saw the inside of a courtroom. He had spent most of his time as a lawyer poring over contracts, a tedious activity that had shaped his mindset. "When does that happen?" he wondered out loud, drawing Lorna closer to him on the brown leather couch in her apartment. When does a breach of contract become serious enough to dissolve the contract? When had Vanessa dissolved their contract? With the first affair? With the tenth? Was Don expected to stay in the marriage for the sake of their vows of "'til death do us part"? Thankfully Vanessa wanted out as well, so it was not an issue. But she played an unexpected card at one point in the divorce proceedings. Vanessa reminded Don that during their first summer together he said to her that he loved her so much that he just wanted her to be happy, and so he would not hold her back if she ever found someone else who made her happier.

Putting her wine glass on the coffee table, Lorna blurted, "You said what?"

"I told her that I loved her so much that I would not stand in the way of her happiness if she found someone else who could make her happier."

Lorna frowned and said, "That's about as romantic as a prenuptial agreement."

Don fell back and away on the couch.

"How can you say that? It was the ultimate gesture of love and romance."

Lorna leaned in. "It was the ultimate gesture of stupidity and self-loathing." She collapsed on his chest in mock exhaustion.

"Oh come on. That's cynical," he said, playfully pushing her away.

"Not at all. That kind of pledge is just the flip side of a prenup. With a prenup you say, 'I love you, but let's be practical. Not all marriages last.' With your self-sacrificing pledge you said 'I love you, but let's be practical. Not all loves last and I'm highly imperfect. So I recognize that you may find someone who makes you happier.'"

Don stood up and walked to the window, wondering to himself whether to continue this conversation. He couldn't let it go.

"Oh come on, Lorna, it's the opposite of a prenup because it's not selfish; it's selfless."

Lorna was enjoying the joust.

"But that's just as bad," she said. "Romantic love isn't practical, and anyone who takes a practical attitude toward it just doesn't get it. And that should bother whoever they're with."

Don bristled and said, "But you're missing the point. It wasn't practical in the sense of seeking protection for myself. It was highly impractical in the sense that I didn't ask her to reciprocate. I told Vanessa that I couldn't imagine ever being with anyone but her."

Lorna arched an eyebrow.

"But you could imagine her being with someone other than you?"

Don's shoulders drooped. "Of course."

"Why?"

Don looked at the ceiling. "I had put her on a pedestal."

Lorna crooked her neck back to look up at him from the couch. "Exactly. Do you think she liked the view from the pedestal?"

"What do you mean?"

Lorna got up and pushed Don down to the couch, standing above him. "Here's what she saw from there: a man who didn't feel secure enough about himself to believe that she could feel about him the way he felt about her. That's not a nice view. She would have alternated between suspecting you of wanting her to reciprocate the pledge and despising you for not feeling her equal."

"You're giving Vanessa too much credit. She didn't think about these things."

"Maybe so. But she felt them, Don."

Lorna collapsed on the couch next to Don.

"How do you know?"

"How did she react when you made your pledge? Did she reciprocate?"

"No."

"Did she seem pleased? Flattered?"

"I assumed that's how she felt because that's how I intended her to feel. I can't imagine she felt any other way."

"Try imagining a little harder." Lorna gave Don a knowing look, and before he could respond she continued, "Did she act flattered? Did she tell you that she told her friends, and they all envied her for having the most romantic boyfriend?"

"No."

"What exactly did she say when you made that pledge?"

"She said something like, 'Don't say that. You know I'll always love you. You'll always make me happy.'"

"How did you respond?"

"I repeated the pledge."

"How did she respond?"

"She told me again not to say that. But I took that as her being modest."

"She was annoyed, Don. No woman wants to hear that her man is willing to give her up if she can do better. A woman wants to hear that a man will fight for her no matter what."

"That's a bit antiquated, isn't it?"

"Maybe, but it's still true. A woman wants men to compete over her, and she wants the winner to claim her as a prize he refuses to live without. A man who suggests that he would let her go is not fully a man. She can't fully respect him. She may say she does; she may even tell herself she does. But she doesn't."

"All right, but those things changed when we got married. It wasn't part of the wedding vows that she could leave if she found someone better."

Lorna finished her glass of wine and poured more. Don's glass was untouched.

"Of course not. But, Don, if pledging that you could leave if you find someone better was the height of romantic love, wouldn't that be part of the wedding vows?"

"Well, not necessarily, since wedding vows go back to a property conception of marriage, long before people married for love…"

Lorna cut him off, saying, "Yeah, yeah, but things have changed, and people write their own vows these days. Of all the goofy self-authored vows you've heard, have you ever heard vows that pledged 'All I want is your happiness, and if you ever find another who can give you happiness better than I can, you should forsake me for that other?'"

"No, of course not."

"That's right, because marriage is a commitment to make things work even if there are better or more attractive alternatives."

"You seem to know a lot about marriage for someone who's never been married."

"I've had sex with a lot of married guys."

"Touché."

Lorna raised her glass in mock salute.

"So are you saying I'm to blame for Vanessa's infidelity?"

"Partly. She couldn't properly respect or trust you after you made your little pledge. She couldn't reciprocate it, and you would have protested if she did. Even before you got married, your romantic love probably had started to fade. It always does. And so that pledge, which was silly and sentimental at the time, became threatening because you would eventually want the same escape clause. And in any event, you were not the warrior who won her hand against a rival. You were just some lucky schmo who was ready to lay down in defeat if a superior rival appeared."

Don winced and took a drink. "So are you saying I was responsible for the divorce?"

"Vanessa should have tried to make things work with you instead of sleeping around. But since she never fully respected you, it's partly your fault."

"Do you think she was serious when she mentioned my pledge?"

"No, of course not. Something you said when you were in love at twenty-two doesn't count when you're getting divorced at fifty-two. She didn't think she had a right to sleep around. But she still felt shortchanged that she hadn't been won by a warrior who would not let her go."

Don gulped his wine. "I don't know, maybe."

Lorna drew him closer by his shirt collar. "The funny thing is that you're not that way at all now. You're not sappy. You're not insecure or self-loathing. I wouldn't spend a minute with you if you were."

"I guess that I learned. Vanessa never validated me. So I learned to validate myself."

Don pushed her down on the couch and got on top.

"Good boy," she said.

* * *

Andy Johnson came in third in the election. For three weeks after, he moped around the house in his coffee-stained light blue bathrobe. When he went to the office he had trouble focusing. His fingers kept hitting the wrong numbers on the calculator. "What did you think was going to happen?" his wife Sally asked. "Even if you had won, so what?" She was right. Vermont wanted change, but Vermont did not want his change. The SVR's anti-corporate message, their radical environmentalism, their social engineering—these were the things that appealed to disaffected Vermonters. Johnson and Free Vermont weren't selling what they wanted.

# 5

The phone startled Don. He picked up with his usual interrogative "Hello?"

"Hi Dad. Were you napping?"

"No, just playing *Tetris*."

"I can't believe you still play that game."

"I like what I like, Deborah."

"Well, would you like to come to see the kids' school concert next Tuesday?"

"Sure. You can get me at the train station, right?"

"Of course, Dad. Plan to stay for dinner. The boys would love to see you after school."

"Great. We can play some ball in the backyard."

"Dad, you know neither one of them really likes to play ball. But Lex has football for his video-game console."

"Ah, yeah, OK, maybe I'll teach them how to play *Tetris*."

Don caught the Metro North train from Grand Central Station to Hastings. He marveled at how clean and safe the terminal felt. The brass gleamed, and the panhandlers kept their distance. Somehow the city had lost its edge.

Don was always glad to attend events involving his grandchildren. He liked soccer games in particular because they were easier to watch than baseball games. Soccer seemed pretty simple — you try to kick the ball in the other team's goal. Baseball was complicated, both in its rules and in its skills, and for that reason it was painful to watch eight-year-olds playing. Tee ball for the five- and six-year-olds was cute. They could all hit the ball off the tee and run. The coach-pitch game of the seven-year-olds was tolerable, because the coaches put the ball over the plate for the kids to hit. Not all of them could hit, of course, and very few could field, but it was watchable. By contrast, the first few years of the kids pitching to one another were sheer misery to watch. The pitchers couldn't find the plate, the batters couldn't hit, and the fielders couldn't make a simple infield putout. Actually, each team had a few stars who could do it all: hit, pitch, and field—and do it well. But his grandsons were not among those stars. It wasn't fair, though, to look at your kids or grandkids through the lens of your own childhood. Sports had been everything to Don as a kid, and so he had been among the stars of the team—or at least that's how he remembered it.

Anyway, this was the kind of school assembly he always enjoyed. Each class had a song to sing, and the little ones were cute. Don's grandkids, Lex and Ben, weren't doing anything special, just singing songs they had over-rehearsed with their classmates, but it would still fill him with pride to see the boys on stage. They were doing something that any normal child could do and yet it was inspiring. By contrast, when they struck out in a baseball game it made him cringe even though they were just doing what every other normal kid was doing. Don wondered how the parents and grandparents of the stars felt. Were they inordinately proud of their little prodigies? Did they take their performance for granted? Did they despise the weakness and ineptitude of the other kids? Don would have.

The assembly began with a false-sounding welcome from the principal and a few announcements—there would be a PTA meeting next Wednesday and a bake sale the following Friday. Then there was the Pledge of Allegiance. All stood at attention with hands on heart, facing the flag, chanting in unison:

*I pledge allegiance*
*to the flag*
*of the United States of America*
*and to the Republic*
*for which it stands*
*One nation*

*under God*
*indivisible*
*with liberty and justice for all.*

Like a prayer that you memorized before you knew what the words meant, the pledge had the eerie quality of commitment without comprehension. Don had no screaming objections to "one nation under God." It was a bit of harmless, antiquated rhetoric, as far as he was concerned. But, as he listened to these children saying what they did not understand, he was struck by the oddity of pledging allegiance to a flag. He had never understood the sanctity of the flag to some people. *But maybe it starts young with the pledge? Surely, anyone who has served in the military, especially during times of war, comes to revere the flag. They seem to forget, though, that it's only a symbol.*

Don knew he should stop this train of thought. He was there to enjoy a school assembly, not to construct a mental manifesto. He needed his *Tetris* game, but he couldn't start playing it now. Could he? Instead, he squirmed in his seat and tried to focus on how cute his grandsons looked in their uniforms. When that didn't work, he searched the auditorium for eye candy. There was a redhead three rows in front and to the right. She had the look of the recently divorced woman advertising for a new mate in high heels, black skirt too tight, and white blouse too low. Were those fake breasts? They had to be. Too round and firm for a woman in her thirties.

It was no use. The kids had finished the pledge, but Don wasn't done and the redhead wasn't working. Despite himself, he continued to muse: *There is no oath of citizenship for those of us born in the United States. Immigrants must swear an oath, but the rest of us don't. That was an intentional part of the setup thanks to John Locke, who was a major influence on the Founding Fathers. Locke maintained that we were born citizens of no country and that we only became citizens by giving our consent to be governed.*

*Why is it, then, that no one ever asks native-born Americans to give their consent to be governed by the United States of America? Did anyone ever ask that redhead? No, that's because there are two kinds of consent according to Locke, stated and tacit. Stated consent is the kind that immigrants give when they swear an oath. Tacit consent comes when a person accepts the benefits of citizenship. It's understood that if you're accepting the benefits of citizenship, like voting and police protection and the court system, that you also accept the limitations that come with citizenship in the form of being governed and obeying the laws of the land.*

*Here these kids are being made to pledge allegiance. It doesn't count as stated consent because they aren't old enough for it to count, and it doesn't even count for the adults who are saying it because this is not an official ceremony like a wedding—you can say the wedding vows all you want, but that doesn't make you married unless it's part of an official wedding ceremony. Still, these kids get the experience of declaring their allegiance and willingness to be governed from kindergarten on. Jefferson would have been horrified.*

*"Indivisible." Ninety percent of these kids think this means "invisible." Half of them are probably even saying "invisible." Who knows what sense they make of that? God is invisible and he's mentioned in the pledge, so maybe it makes sense to think that the "Republic" for which the flag stands is invisible too. The few kids who know what "indivisible" means probably think that it's a very good thing. Unlike their families, half of which have been broken by divorce, their country cannot be broken.*

There was a desperate housewife one row up and to the left with a healthy mane of dark brown hair. Her sweat pants suggested she was concealing the expanse of hips and thighs that reacted to the slightest indulgence in chocolate—no way to fit into her favorite jeans today. That was all right. Her skin was flawless and the whites of her eyes gleamed in a way that reminded Don of Lorna. But then the overly tall woman next to her shifted to block Don's view, returning him to Locke's point that tacit consent can be withdrawn. *Someone who has not sworn an oath of liberty but who has simply drifted into a relationship of being governed can withdraw anytime. No hard feelings. It's like a couple who decide to move in together without getting married. There is no formal commitment, and so if they decide that the arrangement is no longer working for them, they can call it off. For Jefferson and the founders, this was emphatically not an "indivisible" nation. It was a group of states that had come together.*

The fifth grade was singing about the seasons. There was no way to enjoy that without one of your kids on stage, and he still couldn't see the MILF in sweatpants. Don's thoughts returned unbidden: *The original Constitution, before the 14th Amendment, contained no prohibition against a state seceding. And in fact, the original state constitutions of New York, Virginia, and Rhode Island explicitly asserted their right to leave the Union if they wanted to. It was only after the Civil War that the right of secession was formally denied to the states. Sheer hypocrisy. This country actually began with a civil war. We don't frame it that way for school children like those fifth graders singing about autumn's grandeur and winter's sleep. We teach it as a great revolution in which a tyrannical monarchy was overthrown. Yes, that's what it was, but it was also a civil war in which fellow citizens fought against one another.*

"Be quiet, Dad!"

Without realizing it, Don had begun sharing his thoughts with Deborah.

"We can talk about it later, Dad," she said.

Under other circumstances Deborah would have enjoyed the chance to discuss politics. But the stares and shushes of people around them made clear that this was not the time and place.

"You're embarrassing me, Dad."

Unable to restrain himself, Don left in a huff and took a taxi to the train station.

Back in his empty apartment, he began banging out ideas for a blog. If you didn't like the soda law in New York City you were free to move somewhere else without the law. In that way, the fifty states and many municipalities provided options, but the real options were pretty few, actually. If you thought the federal income tax was unjust, as Andy Johnson did, you were out of luck. You were welcome to leave the country, since tacit consent could be withdrawn. You were not held captive by the United States, and that seemed to justify a great deal. You could love it or leave it. *"The problem is that there isn't anywhere else to go. In nearly all ways America is your best option. So it's a bit like being on a ship at sea and being told that you're free to leave the ship anytime you want if you don't like the rules. Since the alternative is jumping into the ocean, you're pretty much stuck with the rules of the ship."* Of course, as the kids at the assembly would learn, you are free to work within the democratic system to change the rules. That is what good Americans have done for generations, but now some people were no longer satisfied with the slow progress. Americans were trying to pull the country in opposite directions. Johnson and Free Vermont had some important common ground with the SVR, but ultimately they wanted government to play very different roles. So while they fought it out, the system persisted. Something new was needed.

The next morning, sipping tea at her desk, Lorna laughed at the pledge blog. She could just picture Don losing his cool as the thoughts occurred to him, and she loved the way he connected the dots. The comments rolled in. Many were screaming denunciations of Don as a "commie atheist bent on the destruction of America," but others actually amplified Don's message. A reader from Nebraska pointed out that the author of the pledge was a Christian socialist minister, and a reader from Kansas shed light on the history of the hand-on-heart gesture. It turns out that the original salute involved extending one's arm at an upward angle at the flag. This was changed after Hitler came to power because it closely resembled the "Heil Hitler" salute. An atheist reader from New Mexico pointed out that even though a Christian minister had written the pledge in 1892 the phrase "under God" wasn't included. It wasn't until 1954, at the height of the Red Scare, that "under God" was officially added to the pledge as a way of distinguishing this country from the godless communists.

The final reply was from John Mackey: "Come to North Dakota. There are only 700,000 people living on 70,000 square miles."

"What are you talking about?" Don asked.

# 6

Where would he get the money? Don's divorce settlement had him awake. He knew he should have listened to his lawyer and fought harder, but at the time he just wanted it all to be over. Now there was nothing he could do. Counting sheep didn't help, and his *Tetris* game was in the living room. To move his mind off his own matters Don began contemplating the ways contracts could hurt people who weren't even parties to the contracts. How could contracts bind future generations? The Constitution was a contract made generations ago and yet kept in force for succeeding generations who never agreed to it.

Unable to restrain himself, Don nudged Lorna awake and began vocalizing his thoughts. "Jefferson wouldn't believe it. He thought it would be a good thing to have a revolution every twenty years. Each generation should have the experience of writing its own constitution. Of course, with that kind of instability a nation could not survive and prosper."

"Go back to sleep, Don."

"I can't."

Lorna rolled over to face Don, but she kept her eyes closed.

Don continued, "The right to rebel, the right to change things, ultimately the right to secede is implicit in the Constitution itself. It was not intended to be a sacred document binding people for all time. It was a provisional agreement that people could accept or reject. The Constitution allows for its own abolition and has its own implicit opt-out clause."

Despite Lorna's distaste for the legal profession, her ears perked up when Don talked about the Constitution, even when he woke her in the middle of the night. She resented anything that bound people in place, including golden handcuffs. Lorna had been working as a summer associate at Wright and Chase after her second year of law school when she discovered that senior partners routinely spent thousands of dollars for sex with high-end call girls. Intrigued, she had frank discussions with her male colleagues about which escort services were best and why. When Lorna left Wright and Chase to work at Red Cap she was never more than a thousand-dollar girl, but she learned the business from all angles. Two years later she started Elite Encounters with some of the best talent from Red Cap and rival agencies.

"What if your employees had to sign a contract?" Don asked.

Lorna opened her eyes and adjusted her head on the pillow. "My girls are not bound to me," she said. "They're free to come or go. Pimps use force, intimidation, and drugs to keep girls subservient and stupid. Me, I give respect, fair terms, and an open door. Girls stay because they want to, and they leave when they want to."

"Yeah, but imagine if daughters were bound to prostitution because of a promise their mothers had made before the daughters were born," Don said.

Lorna sat up a little, saying, "Of course. There are places like that in India, where girls are born to be prostitutes and promised to pimps. It makes the Indian girls with arranged marriages look lucky."

"Right," Don said, turning on the light. "The thing is that we're misled into thinking that we were born into a scenario that binds us to an either-or choice between citizenship or leaving for another country. We're told that we can't stay in place and leave at the same time."

Lorna squinted. "That's not fair."

"Exactly," Don said. "Because the Fourteenth Amendment is bullshit."

"What do you mean?"

"It's like a clause in a marriage contract added by the husband saying that neither party can ever leave the marriage. If the wife is forced to sign, it can't be valid."

"True," she said.

Don got out of bed.

"Where are you going?"

"I think I'll play some *Tetris*."

"Turn off the light, and do it in the other room. I need to get back to sleep."

# 7

Dakota was bright. You could see forever as the prairie expanded in all directions, but the effect was unsettling. What could you see? There was nothing in any direction, so it felt like you were stuck. No matter how far you drove, the scenery remained the same. A look at the map reassured Don that geographical change was beyond the horizon. Before meeting Mackey outside Fargo, he took a detour west to the badlands and Roosevelt National Park with its rocky, otherworldly terrain. The wild horses made sense of it all. Don had never even thought of horses as wild animals. They seemed to need people to take care of them and ride them, as if their natural habitat was a farm. But here they were running free, no stable to go home to at night, no one to feed or shoe them, no one to assist with the birth of their foals. Yet apparently they were fine. It all seemed natural until Don recalled that the horses were not native to North America. They had been brought here by the Spanish. The horses he saw were descendants of horses that had escaped and made a new home. Yet even here they were protected within the confines of a national park. Their numbers had dwindled, and their safety was government-secured. Still, when Don saw them running free, no saddles, no riders, nowhere to go, he could imagine the wild horses from which the Spanish horses had descended. The horse may be domesticated, but it is essentially a wild animal, unlike the dog, which bears scant resemblance to the wolf from which it was bred. It was a bold and ingenious move for people to tame and ride horses, but the wild animal has not been erased.

Less impressive were the bison, simply because Don expected to see them at Roosevelt National Park and because they had never lost their appearance as a wild animal. In recent years, bison have been farm raised for their lean meat, but that always seemed like something of a joke to Don. The meat lacks the fat that flavors beef, and it costs more. When you see one of those giant animals corralled, you know it's not meant to be. The wooly head would have been bred out generations ago in a truly domesticated animal. At Roosevelt National Park, Don saw a stampede, but it was a poor thing compared to the picture in his imagination of bison thundering across the planes, hunted by whooping Sioux. It was as if these specimens were being kept in a museum out of pity and curiosity. They would be nobler if they could no longer be seen.

Mackey lived in Akston, home to 700 residents and one traffic light, an hour north of Fargo. Driving distances were relative. Dakotans thought of an hour the way that Don thought of ten minutes. Everything was stretched out and expanded. The land was flat and the people pleasant. Along with an impressive number of Native Americans, there were lots of round, blonde people, mostly descended from Germans and Norwegians and Danes and Swedes. The young people stepped from the pages of a fitness catalog, but their diet was unkind to their aging. Svelte teenage girls became roly-poly middle-aged moms. For days, Don hadn't heard a contrary word, but that made him uncomfortable.

The long drive back from Roosevelt National Park led the red Camaro across the prairie to Mackey. His hair was dark and his complexion was Mediterranean, black Irish. One of his shoulders was higher than the other, and his head tilted right to compensate for a slight scoliosis. "You Jenkins?" he asked as Don got out of the car.

"That's me, John. You sure have a beautiful state. I just spent a couple of days at Roosevelt National Park and..."

"Call me Mackey," he interrupted.

"All right, Mackey."

"Where's your bags? In the trunk? Let's grab 'em and get inside before we freeze our asses off."

Mackey led them into the den, a dark space with a TV-VCR

combination and a shag carpet. Over cans of Old Milwaukee, Don learned that Mackey was a renegade Catholic. He had studied for the priesthood at the seminary in Fargo but left after two years. "There were no hard feelings. There was no pledge. They didn't want you if you didn't want them," he said. As desperate as the Church was for priests, they didn't want Mackey. "I asked too many questions, had too little respect for authority." So he was free to go in all good graces. "It's like that at West Point too," he told Don. "You can stay for a couple of years and then leave without owing them anything. But if you stay and graduate you owe them big time. You're committed to service."

Mackey explained that he met Mary while working in the library at North Dakota State University, where he split his time between shelving books and daydreaming. "I was floundering, didn't know what to do with myself. Just thinking a lot without doing anything. Mary and me got married and she pushed me to open the diner." Mary had been waiting tables at Lorenzo's. The place was a mistake, jarred sauce and chewy pasta, but the sassy blonde waitress with the prominent derriere made Mackey a regular.

He knew the business, had worked in diners and restaurants as a teenager and all through college until he went into the seminary. No one wanted to stay at those jobs. Everyone had a plan. Mackey's plan was to become a priest, but in the seminary he had never stopped thinking and talking about his time working as a bus boy, waiter, and fry cook. Time disappeared when he worked. It wasn't pure pleasure, especially in the moment. It wasn't like much of anything in the moment, and that was the point. It was absorbing and challenging in just the right mix. Mackey wasn't anyone's idea of Dakota-nice, but that made him all the more effective as a waiter in the no-nonsense atmosphere of a busy eatery. He knew what people wanted and he affirmed them with a nod, "The meatloaf, good choice."

Mary's dream was to have her own place, and nowadays she

does. Mackey's Diner was an old steel trolley on Main Street in Akston that had been closed for years when the Mackeys bought it from the bank. The ceilings were low and the quarters were cramped. Red vinyl upholstered the booths and the stools, three of which had been torn and repaired with gray duct tape. Mackey liked it that way, and so it remained despite Mary's desire for a polished new start. "The customer is always right because we never do wrong." That's what Mary taught their employees, a motley bunch of first-opportunity and second-chance folks, like Renata, whose entanglement with a Mexican cartel got her a stint at a women's prison in Colorado. Mackey had hired Renata on the spot. She didn't have to tell him anything. He knew.

The jawing people did at the counter was mostly bullshit, but it wasn't pure bullshit. Sometimes it concealed truth, hurt, pain—and Mackey could see right through to it. People didn't want to reveal too much of themselves, and they would often say the opposite of what they meant. It wasn't quite irony, certainly not sarcasm. It was veiled unveiling. A few weeks ago Joe "the Crow" Cronauer switched to decaf and Mackey joshed with him about giving up booze too. Joe the Crow made an offhand remark about porn, and Mackey knew the guy's real problem. A glance told the Crow that Mackey understood, no judgment, no guilt.

"People want to reveal themselves, but you have to listen," Mackey told Don. Don scratched his stubble and began to reply, but Mackey continued, "I guess it's more a talent than a skill. I didn't even realize I had the talent until I saw how much other people didn't have it when I was working with other seminarians and priests at a homeless shelter in Fargo. Homeless people don't want to tell you their true story. Instead, they give you a bullshit story with just a hint or two of truth. They hope you'll pick up on the truth, but your ability to pick up on that truth is also a test of whether or not they think you're worthy of hearing it."

Don balanced his beer and leaned forward in the brown lounger, "I would've thought priests and seminarians would be good at that, John...I mean Mackey."

"Fucking idiots. Sometimes it was hard to believe they meant well, but they did. They really did." The priests and other seminarians would focus on some part of the story that to Mackey was obviously false and ignore the detail that was crucial—the one that revealed this woman was fleeing an abusive man, or the detail that revealed this man had legal problems that kept him from feeling safe in telling his true story.

Don sank back in the chair and sipped warm beer as the stories continued. Mackey was a magnet. That much was clear. People didn't know it, didn't admit it, but they came to Mackey to confess and to be offered absolution for what were not sins. His counter was his confessional and he demanded no penance, no acts of contrition. He offered affirmation instead. Larry Hartfield wanted to leave his wife. He wasn't just bitching and moaning in the usual coffee-shop way. This wasn't "take my wife, please." This was talking about his job while all the while really talking about his wife. Mackey never suggested a course of action. He would just talk about something he had done. So he told Larry about how he left the seminary and told him it had been the best decision he ever made. Two months later Larry was divorced. Six months later Larry was working as a fisherman in Florida.

Over the next three weeks at Mackey's Diner and in Mackey's home, Don witnessed it all for himself. Mackey had never been interested in politics, but from listening to the counter customers, slowly over the years he had gotten interested in what he called anti-politics. He was now the unofficial leader of Free North Dakota. The group was clearly interested in expanding, yet Mackey said nothing of it. Don had expected the hard-sell but he got the no-sell. Instead, one day Mackey threw him an apron.

"Make yourself useful," he said.

"What do you want me to do?"

"Start by pouring coffee. You can do that, can't you?"

# 8

Chuck Larson sat at the counter where Renata took his order, "Two eggs sunny side up, and bacon," he said. The stainless steel of the coffee maker gleamed as Don grabbed a fresh pot and poured a cup for Larson.

Larson took off his John Deere cap. Speaking to no one in particular, he said, "You people are just greedy. You want it all for yourself. But things don't work that way. You have to share, you have to be community-minded."

Mackey turned around behind the counter to face Larson and put down his spatula. "Envy is worse than greed," Mackey said. "Greed is the seed of self-destruction, but envy is the cancer of society."

"That makes no sense. Greed is greed," Larson said.

Mackey walked down to Larson's seat at the counter. The clinking of silverware ceased. On the radio Geddy Lee sang about philosophers and ploughmen. Don lowered the volume so everyone could hear.

Mackey looked Larson in the eye, saying, "People do stupid things out of greed, but most of that greed comes from envy. We see that someone has more than we do, and we want more because if that guy has it then we must deserve it too. Envy is reciprocity gone wrong. It's looking at the product instead of the process. It's demanding more be done for me and given to me because some unseen and undetected violation of reciprocity must have resulted in unequal distribution."

Larson scowled, stirred his coffee, and then clanked his spoon on the dish. Renata brought his breakfast, the bacon still sizzling from the grill. He stabbed a piece and put it in his mouth, saying, "No, Mackey. Greed leads to inequality. The more greed, the more inequality, and the more inequality, the more unstable the society."

"Depends on what you mean by inequality, Larson. We're all equal before the law, but there it stops. We're not all equal in talents and abilities, and so we're not equal in prizes and possessions."

With egg dripping from his chin, Larson replied, "Sure, not everyone has to have exactly the same, but you can't just let the system run unchecked. Government needs to redistribute to keep things fair."

Mackey half-smiled and closed his eyes for a moment before saying, "The nation of North Dakota will not correct for natural inequalities. The government will not play Robin Hood, because, unlike King John, the rich will have done nothing wrong in acquiring their wealth. Robbing from the rich to give to the poor is just as unfair as when the rich rob the poor. In fact, it's worse because it stops the spillover effect that makes a whole society wealthy."

Shaking his head, Larson replied, "It's not about who deserves what, Mackey. It's about taking care of people in need and not allowing some people to have so much money and power that others have none."

"Society is not a family," Mackey replied. "The family is the place for socialism, for taking care of people who have not earned or deserved it."

Larson ran his hand through his thick blonde hair. "So that's it, huh Mack? Just take care of your own."

"No, Chuck, it's just that the family is the only place where there's a real obligation. Outside that it becomes voluntary."

"Yeah, but no one's gonna volunteer."

"Not true, Chuck. Glen Summers is setting up his charity. People are willing to give money to provide a safety net. It's just that people want to give rather than have the money taken from them."

"You can't just leave it up to people how much to give and who to give it to. Everyone needs to have a vote on how much to tax the rich and how to use the money."

"You know the old saying, Chuck, 'The problem with socialism is that sooner or later you run out of other people's money.'"

Larson stood up. "That's not fair, Mackey. You know I'm not talking about socialism."

"No, not pure socialism—just the kind we have in the United States today."

Larson opened his wallet and put a five-dollar bill on his plate. "You people are un-American," he said, waving both hands to encompass the counter, before turning around and walking out the door. Don turned up the music and the percussion of silverware resumed.

The FND plan was simple: people who want personal and economic liberty in a combination that neither Republicans nor Democrats are willing to offer have a right to come together and form their own country. States have the right to secede. North Dakota is virtually unpopulated, and so people could move there and secede. The FND website laid out the plan. Since there were not enough North Dakotans interested in FND, the invitation had been issued to all Americans. At this point, five years had passed and over five thousand people from fifteen states had moved to North Dakota. Most of these first five thousand were consultants and other self-employed people whose work was highly portable, but the increase in population would surely increase demand for houses and infrastructure. Once a critical mass was hit, small business owners, independent contractors, and everyone else needed to service the growing population would follow.

FND had always operated under the assumption that its communications were being monitored, but now there was a federal agent snooping around. He had even come to the meetings, this Webster Daniels. Daniels made no threats, but his presence was felt. Mackey's view had always been that FND should operate with complete transparency. So there was precious little for Daniels to learn at meetings that he couldn't have learned from clicking around the website. There was no membership list. To keep track of their swelling numbers, though, Mackey asked new members to let him know how many voting-age members there were in their family.

\* \* \*

"It's a takeover," Webster Daniels told the natives. He wasn't making anything up. FND's website plainly stated its secessionist aim and its invitation to people from other states to move to North Dakota to help accomplish this aim. "How *free* will North Dakota be when a bunch of out-of-staters start running things?" he'd ask. That was enough to agitate Jack Klosterman, the mayor of Fargo. Attracted by Mackey, a good percentage of the recent immigrants had moved in and around Fargo. Grateful for this boon to the economy, the mayor had ignored the fact that these folks saw themselves as in the business of putting the government out of business.

"Live and let live, that's my philosophy," Mayor Klosterman told Agent Daniels.

Leaning back in his seat at Kelly's Steak House, Daniels said, "That's a fine philosophy, a pragmatic philosophy, an American philosophy. Unless..." Daniels cut into his rib eye and began to chew.

"Unless what?" Klosterman asked, leaning forward.

Daniels finished chewing and took a long drink from his frosty mug, before replying, "Unless they represent a credible threat."

\* \* \*

Ronnie Black paused to survey the diner through dark

sunglasses after the tinkling bells announced his arrival. Finding his preferred seat at the end of the counter occupied, Ronnie hovered at the end, drinking a cup of coffee. In a few moments the man in overalls hastily abandoned his remaining toast and eggs. Ronnie sat down and pushed the plate aside before Mary Mackey could clear it. "All the phones are tapped, you know." The counter fell silent. When no one replied Ronnie continued, "Daniels is a decoy."

"Really?" said a man in a flannel jacket.

"That's right," said Ronnie. "The feds have infiltrated FND."

"So who can we trust?" Bert Connors asked.

"Trust no one but number one."

"Thanks Ronnie," Bert replied.

With that, Ronnie Black rose, put two dollars on the counter and walked out the door. He had repeated this act every day for the past two weeks. The first few times it lasted much longer, but then Bert Connors discovered that if he asked Ronnie who they can trust that would allow Ronnie to deliver his signature line, "Trust no one but number one." And they would all be free of him momentarily.

\* \* \*

Don began blogging about North Dakota. He described the folks who had come to North Dakota as being *"like people who have just seen an emotionally compelling movie. They nod in assent and recognition of one another without a need to say anything about it."* They were connected by their pursuit of freedom and their confidence that they could achieve it in numbers. Don's blog described the nod as the *"symbolic gesture of the movement. Not in-your-face like the peace sign, just the self-contained simple nod. It is at once a combination of self-assurance and a bow to the principles embodied in the other person. It has not replaced the handshake as a greeting, but whenever two FND members encounter one another there is the nod. The effect is especially powerful when the people recognize one another from FND but have never been formally introduced. A chatty self-introduction is unnecessary. The nod says it all, says, 'I understand what you understand.'"*

# 9

"Undress," she said, "and put this around your neck."

His suit a wrinkled mass on the floor, Glen Summers stood at erect attention while she attached the chain to his collar.

"Dogs don't stand," she said.

"I'm sorry," he said.

"They don't talk either. Bark for me."

"Ruff ruff."

"Good boy. Now let's take a little walk."

He panted as he crawled behind her.

She flicked her raven mane and looked back over her shoulder. "You want to sniff my ass like a good little dog?"

"Ruff ruff."

"Up on your knees and beg."

When the hour was over, a payment in goldens was transferred from his account to hers.

\* \* \*

Backed by actual gold, goldens had become popular as currency among FND members. As the price of gold rose, so did the value of the golden. And with the declining confidence in the dollar worldwide the golden looked set to rise in value for the foreseeable future. Among themselves, then, most FND folks preferred the golden as a means of exchange.

To outsiders, this practice of trading in goldens was disconcerting; it smacked of some kind of religion or cult. Not quite that actually, but rather of some kind of nerdy obsession like speaking Klingon or spending real money to buy game pieces for some massively multiplayer role-playing game. The stuff of Dungeons and Dragons. But as the value of the golden continued to increase, outsiders became intrigued, including the Treasury Department. The government of the United States claims a monopoly on the currency used within its borders, and Glen Summers was undermining that monopoly.

\* \* \*

Six years after the birth of FND, Mackey's prediction proved correct, as independent contractors and small-business owners began flocking to the state. With its low tax rates, North Dakota was already a more hospitable environment for business than most other states in the Union. Mackey aimed to swell the ranks of FND to five hundred thousand voters before moving for secession.

The plan for post-secession North Dakota was that there would be no income tax. Instead there would be a per capita tax, an "equal tax." Each family would pay based on the number of adults and children in the family. The amount to be paid would be minimal, just enough to support the night-watchman state. Early estimates suggested that two thousand dollars per head per year would be sufficient. The budget would not dictate taxes; instead, taxes would dictate the budget. FND conceived of taxes as akin to membership dues. An organization must strive to keep membership dues minimal and must provide value in return for dues. Additionally, no member should be charged more in dues than any other member. Fairness did not result from charging each member the same percentage of their income. Why, after all, should income be taxed? The government did nothing to make that income possible. They might as well tax savings or anything else they did nothing to make possible. No, fairness resulted from charging members the same amount for dues. The amount would be considered a pittance for some and a hardship for others, but all would get the same benefits. And if the benefits of living in a society that allowed for maximal freedom were worth it, all would flourish. No handouts, nothing for free, just the chance to succeed. People would be free to leave, of course, and although there would not be a public safety net, there would be private charity. It would be called what it is, charity. If you were not making ends meet and could not pay for medical care, charity would provide it. The government would not provide, because the government would have no money.

The system in North Dakota would let people give directly to those in need without the government coercing them and taking credit. The government would still have a monopoly on the use of force, but they would no longer use force to spread the wealth around. People would be motivated to give to charity because they would not already have given "at the office" through taxes. They would see charity as a civic good. People would be reluctant to take it, because it would be labeled as charity, not entitlement.

Glen Summers had already begun planning a charity that would provide assistance for those who could not pay their equal tax in full. If a family were committed to a life of freedom in North Dakota, then Summers's charity would pay the part of the equal tax they could not come up with on their own. The payment would be considered an interest-free loan and would be renewed on a year-to-year basis as long as the family were productive members of society. Those who were unproductive would not get the loan and would be asked to leave North Dakota.

Summers found no shortage of deep pockets willing to fund the charity. People were benevolent when they were allowed to be generous rather than being compelled to give without credit. What's more, the deep pockets knew that people who had made the commitment to move to North Dakota were committed to making it on their own and would only accept charity as a last resort.

* * *

Because North Dakota bordered another nation, it felt like an exit. Mackey knew this. South Dakota would not have worked as well. Canada, of course, had its own secessionist issues with the Quebecois. The French and English signs you saw as soon as you crossed into Canada bore witness to the weak glue that held the country together. Practically no one could really speak French outside of Quebec, and practically everyone in Quebec spoke English—they had to, much as they resented it. Canada was two different nations culturally, held together by weakness. The Quebecois' drive for independence would well up occasionally; they would even vote on it. And the rest of Canada was willing to let them go. Ultimately, though, the Quebecois did not have the will. They wanted their own country out of vanity, out of a sense of ethnic identity. That can be a powerful motivator when your ethnic identity is being crushed by a colonizer who won't let you go, but that wasn't the case in Canada. Secession succeeds when the difference that motivates it is philosophical, as when the American colonies declared their independence from England. This is what made things so promising for North Dakota, as Mackey saw it. People from different backgrounds were coming together because they shared a philosophy and because they rejected the philosophy that had come to rule the United States.

Native reaction to FND had grown stronger as the movement grew in numbers. At the current rate of increase, FND members would outnumber the natives in three years. Chuck Larson and Mayor Klosterman were perennial guests on talk radio, stirring up fear and resentment. Practically no one objected to the individual members of FND who had moved from other states. Most of the transplants blended in and were assets to the community. Still, the influx had the feeling of a take over, like some science-fiction movie: The aliens come in peace and bring gifts of superior technology, but with the passage of time you begin to suspect that the aliens have an ulterior motive. Only in this case, the FND members were up front with their motive all along: they wanted to increase in numbers until they could win a vote for secession.

Most native North Dakotans did not like the full-scale freedom envisioned by FND that would legalize drugs, prostitution, and gambling. Many could appreciate such freedom in theory, but it belonged in a philosophy classroom, not in the real world where real problems would result. The natives were more committed to America than they were to their marriages or maybe even their churches. Every school child in the state had learned that the great seal of North Dakota includes the motto "Liberty and Union Now and Forever, One and Inseparable." North Dakota became a state on November 2, 1889 with the Civil War still fresh in mind. On the radio talk show circuit, Klosterman was fond of reminding people that according to the North Dakota Constitution Article 1 Declaration of Rights, Section 23, "The State of North Dakota is an inseparable part of the American Union and the Constitution of the United States is the supreme law of the land."

In a brown leather booth at Kelly's Steak House, Agent Webster Daniels broke bread with his native allies, Klosterman and Larson. Daniels cut into his porterhouse and the juice ran red. "This is not just a North Dakota problem, this is an American problem," he said.

Pursing his lips and picking up his knife, Larson said, "Right. We need to nip this in the bud here."

"Agreed," said Klosterman.

Swallowing his steak and leaning back in the booth, Daniels shook his head and peered across the table at the two natives. "They're winning the public-relations war, though," he said.

Putting down his knife and fork, Klosterman asked, "So, how can we change that? How can we win that war?"

Daniels sipped his bourbon and smirked. "Well, we can't do it by telling people what they already know, that FND is planning for secession. We have to tell people something they don't know, something FND has been keeping secret."

Larson leaned forward and put his elbows on the table, saying, "Like the fact that FND wants to take away their social security and other benefits. Like the fact that they would be second-class citizens in a new nation. Like the fact that FND considers them useless and in the way."

"Those aren't really secrets. People just don't care that much because they don't believe it will ever happen," Klosterman said.

Larson turned to face his friend. "So what do you suggest?"

Klosterman looked straight ahead at Daniels. "We need to give them something to fear, a corporate takeover. Glen Summers is connected to the Andyne Corporation. We can tell North Dakotans that FND is just a puppet and Andyne is pulling the strings. People aren't moving here on their own initiative with their own money. They're not really taking any risks. Andyne is funding it all. Andyne will have bought everything and everyone. If they're not stopped, the secession will happen and we'll all be left working for a corporation rather than being citizens of a country."

Larson scrunched up his face. "But how do we sell that message? You can't fit it on a bumper sticker."

"We need a slogan, something for TV commercials and billboards, something people can't refute or dismiss," Daniels said.

"How about 'Andyne will end North Dakota'?" Klosterman said.

Andyne seemed to have its hands in everything, including the energy sector. In fact, Andyne had been encouraging its employees to move to North Dakota. They hadn't opened an office yet, but Andyne employees who were willing to move to North Dakota were allowed to keep their jobs by telecommuting. Andyne wasn't alone among corporations in encouraging employees to move to North Dakota, but Andyne had been the most aggressive in promoting the practice so far. Few jobs really required flesh-and-blood presence anyway. You could Skype into meetings, talk on the phone, and access all the files by computer. Occasionally, employees would be asked to attend meetings in New York, but Andyne would pay for them to fly in and stay in a hotel. Some North Dakota natives had begun to connect the dots, but when the mayor said it and the newspaper printed it, "Andyne will end North Dakota," caught on.

Sitting at the desk in his new apartment in Fargo, Don blogged that *"A slogan doesn't have to be true to catch on; it just has to be sticky. No one thinks they drink Coke because of the advertising; no one thinks they buy a Honda because of the commercial. In fact most people react indignantly to advertisements and think they're less likely to buy the product because they felt insulted by the slogan. So when they do feel the inclination to buy the product they tell themselves a little story, 'I really shouldn't buy this because the advertising is so crass. But thankfully I realize that, and the advertising is playing no part in my decision to buy it.'"*

# 10

Mackey insisted that it would be a classless society. Of course, the United States was already classless from an official standpoint, but that didn't stop politicians and the media from speaking class language. This became Don's latest target on the *Soda Blog*. He asked his readers to consider the three classes that politicians and the media like to speak of: the working class, the middle class, and the rich. "Working class" seemed to imply that others were members of the "leisure class," some idle rich aristocracy. But the reality was that the rich tended to work more hours than the "working class." So the implication was that the nature of the manual or menial labor done by lower-income people qualified them as "working class." Don wrote that *"Of course such labor counts as work, but there is no reason to deny the label of 'work' to the activity of those who type at computer terminals."* Members of the working class were commonly depicted as striving to make it into the middle class, as if there were some barrier to admission or some official demarcation. And the middle class, as the largest group, were constantly pandered to for their votes. They were depicted as the heart of the society and the economy. The rich were always getting the breaks, whereas the middle class were kept down with the burden of heavy taxes and slow growth.

Don wrote that *"The rhetoric is pernicious in its effect, describing a reality that simply does not exist. Unlike other societies and cultures, past and present, America has no class system. You can be born poor and become rich. There are no doors closed to anyone who can make the money to open them. It works both ways. There is no guarantee to anyone born into a wealthy family that they will remain wealthy. There are no dukes and duchesses, no titles or privileges. Yes, wealthy families take care of their own, but that is their right. The great fear and the great lie in the American media and among the chattering class is that if wealth accumulates in a family it will be preserved and passed down forever, giving some people an advantage that others could never hope to compete with. The truth, though, is that in most cases family money is gone in three or four generations. Statistically, Americans lose 90% of inherited wealth by the third generation. Cornelius Vanderbilt amassed a fortune worth more than 100 billion in today's dollars. But 100 years after his death, his 120 descendants did not include even one millionaire. Where does the wealth go? Usually to smart and capable people who produce goods and services that other people want."*

\* \* \*

Sitting at his desk and staring out the window of his apartment in Fargo, Don bent a paperclip. The phone broke his reverie. His agent, Elizabeth, greeted him with the usual pleasantries, before getting to what was on her mind.

"Obviously, you're writing, Don. And that's great. Your profile and your platform have really grown with this blog. The time is right to cash in. What kind of stories do you have in mind? Any character sketches that I can read?"

"I've been meeting a lot of characters in real life, not much time to think about fiction." Don lied. He had been thinking about fiction constantly, but nothing would come out.

"Well, that's great. Write about them. 'All literature is gossip.' Isn't that what Truman Capote said?"

"You would know, Elizabeth. I've never read Truman Capote."

"Well, that's all right. You get the point, don't you? Real life is the best inspiration for fiction. You model your characters on people you know and your plots on things you've seen. You just make them more interesting and leave out the boring parts that make life ordinary. Isn't that what you did when you wrote *Body of Evidence?"*

"Yes, but that was about sensationalizing things, about pumping up the reader, about keeping the pot boiling. It was about entertainment, pure and simple."

"What's wrong with entertainment, Don?"

Don jabbed his palm with the point of the unfolded paper clip. "Nothing, Elizabeth. It's just that I'm bored of it. The formulas and the plot devices get old. It's like watching yet another episode of *Law and Order*. I can't do it anymore."

"Can't or won't?"

"I don't know. Both. I sit there and I push and nothing comes out, just these blogs."

"But you have all of this fresh inspiration. What about the Vermont Republicans and these people in Wyoming? Of course no one wants to read about those places, but you can take some of the personalities and ratchet up the action with high-stakes D.C. politics or New York corporate intrigue."

Don jabbed his palm again. "It's the Second Vermont Republic. And they're not Republicans; they're closer to socialists. And I'm living in North Dakota now, not Wyoming."

"Oh, you know what I mean. I'm sorry. It's not the places that matter; it's the action and events."

"But in real-life things move more slowly and take less dramatic turns than in fiction, and somehow that's actually more interesting."

"So fine, Don. Follow the real-life events, but then condense the action. Leave out the boring parts that the reader skips. You can do that, can't you?"

"Maybe, but it will take time. Tom Wolfe takes years researching his social-criticism novels. If I ever write again, it will take me years to get it all down."

"Oh, don't say that, Don. You need the money now. I know you've been writing, just not showing it to me."

"No, I haven't, not fiction. You've read my blog. That's the only writing I've been able to produce aside from my daily journal."

Don bent the paperclip back and forth.

"Yes, but surely, you've been sketching characters and plots in your journal, Don, like you've always done."

"No, actually, I've been reflecting on ideas, the kind of things that I write about on the blog. It's like I wish I was back in college majoring in philosophy or political science or something."

"Well no one says you can't have ideas in your novel, Don. That's great as long as the plot is riveting and the characters are compelling. Ideas are fine, just don't get preachy. What did the old movie executive say? 'If you want to send a message, use Western Union.'"

"I don't see how I can do it, Elizabeth. Ideas are ideas and stories are stories. If I write a story that's just a vehicle for ideas I'll feel like it's cheating. And I can't just insert ideas into the midst of a story. It would all have to come together naturally, and I just don't see how."

"So just start chronicling the people and events around you. Later you can change the names to protect the innocent, rev up the plot, leave out the boring parts, and cut to the chase. You can do that, can't you, Don?"

The paper clip broke after one last bend.

"Maybe."

"Maybe? Sure you can. We're counting on you."

"Who's counting on me? You and Vanessa?"

"Oh, don't be silly, Don. Your readers and fans are counting on you—and yes, I'm one of your readers and fans. It's been four years since *Unfortunate Intruder*."

"Well, my readers and fans owe me a sabbatical. And Vanessa can do without the alimony payments. Let her take me to court."

"Oh, Vanessa is awful, I know. But how are the grand-children?"

"I don't know. I haven't seen them since Christmas."

"That's what you need, Don. Come back east for a while and see your grandkids. They'll get you writing stories. Children are so creative, natural artists."

"All right, Elizabeth, I'll think about it. Good talking with you. I have to go now, I'm working at the diner."

"Sounds charming. That's where you write?"

"No, that's where I pour coffee for customers."

"I don't understand."

"Well, it's really about spending time with Mackey and the FND crowd."

"Who is Mickey?"

"It's Mackey, and I'll tell you some other time."

Don tossed the remains of the paperclip in the trash can beside his desk.

Lorna had overheard the call and was giggling in the living room. She shouted, "You had two wives. This one just doesn't realize she's been divorced."

"I know. But this one would really scorch the earth if I fired her. She knows about the girls you introduced me to and she would take it public, and that would hurt my daughter."

Don shut off the light at his desk and walked to his office doorway. Looking at Lorna's profile from ten feet away he could barely see her nose, but when she turned to face him it was there, sculpted and slightly upturned.

"Actually, though, Don, it's not a bad idea for you to write about things that've been happening. 'Write what you know,' isn't that what they say? Didn't you do that with the legal thrillers, take ordinary people and cases and make them larger than life?"

Don joined her in the living room, where she sat on the floor in black yoga pants. "Yeah, I guess so, but that was escapism. It was my mid-life crisis. The things that are going on with FND seem too serious to trivialize in a novel."

"Some of it's kind of crazy, though, isn't it? Like, they're really not gonna have public schools?"

"That's the plan. Of course they'll keep the old public-school buildings, and lots of the natives won't want to pay. So in some sense things won't change dramatically for those who don't want them to change. But the one thing that will change right away is that there will be options and competition. As it is now, kids are stuck going to their local public school, but after secession they'll be able to choose. Of course, most parents and children won't want to travel great distances to go to a different school, but that will at least be a possibility."

Lorna stretched. Her abundant hips and thighs were delightfully out of proportion with her tiny waist. "Competition is good, Don. But people need to have money if competition is going to work. Some of the states have voucher programs where you can take your money shopping for a school. But beggars can't be choosers, and most of these kids will be beggars. They'll just be stuck with whatever school will take them."

Don leaned against the doorway and scratched his neck. "Not so. Even beggars will have choices in Free North Dakota, at least when it comes to schools. Geography may restrict how widely they're willing to shop, but there will be no shortage of schools willing to take them."

"But you're counting on wealthy people to fund schools for others."

"That's right."

"But won't most people be greedy and keep their money for themselves instead of using it to support schools and supplement the education of others? Isn't that human nature?"

"Sure, some people will be that way. But education is a common good, like clean air and water. Everyone wants it. An educated citizenry provides an educated and self-sufficient work force. So it's worth contributing voluntarily to the education of others."

"Sure, Don, in theory. But in practice won't most people just stand by and wait for someone else to be the great benefactor?"

Don sat on the raggedy couch and looked down at Lorna. "'Free riders,' that's what you're talking about. People will want to take advantage of the system and so no one will do anything."

Lorna pulled her hair back in a ponytail, exposing her neck and blonde roots, saying, "Exactly. I'd be a fool to give money to educate someone else's kids if I can count on someone else giving the money. But if everyone counts on everyone else to give the money, then no one gives the money—and the kids don't get educated."

Don thought she sounded maternal, but he kept on point, replying, "The classic example is an old port town that would benefit from having a lighthouse."

Lorna got up and joined him on the couch. "Yeah, Don, I remember the example from law school. It would benefit the sailors, the port workers, the merchants, and nearly everyone else at least indirectly. There are so many people who have an interest in building the lighthouse that it seems silly to tax people to do it. It seems like someone or some group will step up and build the lighthouse. But no one does. That's what I'm talking about. It's fine in theory to think that people will fund education for those who can't or won't pay for education, but the responsibility gets so dispersed that no one steps up. And then you're sunk or without light."

Lorna removed the ponytail holder and her blonde hair fell gently on her bare shoulders. She rested her case. Don was sure that she could have won over any jury in the world. She almost had him convinced.

"The lighthouse case is compelling."

"Yes it is." She smiled, her teeth gleaming.

"But did you know that there's not a single historical case of a town that needed or wanted a lighthouse that didn't get one? Someone or some group always steps up. There is glory and pride to be had in building the lighthouse."

Lorna sunk back in the couch and her eyes widened.

Don continued, "Just think, who will the schools be named after? Benefactors. People like to put their names on things. People like to be recognized. Infrastructure is crumbling across the states. Government can't get it together to fix the roads and bridges because they waste so much money on other projects. But what if they sold or rented the bridges and roads to private companies?"

Lorna scrunched her nose as if she had smelled something rotten. "Oh come on, Don, that's crazy."

"Really, they've done it in France of all places—let private companies like Cofiroute build express roads. That helps everyone, the people who pay the premium rate to take the express roads and the people who stay on the regular roads, which now have reduced traffic thanks to the express roads."

She tightened her lips and shook her head. "But that's just a small example."

"It is, Lorna. But instead of waiting around for government to fix the bridge, why not sell or lease it to a private company who can run things more efficiently, sell naming rights to the bridge and sell advertising on the bridge? Same with the roads. They don't need to be toll roads to make money. They can be named, and advertising space can be sold. Competition. There are any number of companies who would love to have a chance to run the roads and bridges. And if we're squeamish about giving them ownership, we can just rent to them. We don't need the government to *build that,* and we don't need government hovering over us asking for thanks and taxes because of what they built. It's just a failure of imagination to think otherwise."

Lorna leaned back and rolled her head side to side. "Maybe, Don. But you're a writer. Don't you think you let your imagination get away from you a bit?"

"Look what's happened to communications," he said, gesturing to the window. "Previous generations thought we needed the government to deliver the mail and safeguard a monopoly for the phone company. And look what happened when the government got out of the way just a little and allowed competition. Would we have cheap overnight package delivery if the post office were our only option? Would we have cheap mobile-phone service if the phone company were still a monopoly? Of course not. So if we want better roads, bridges, and schools, we need government to get out of the way."

Lorna leaned in, saying, "Maybe, Don, maybe. But what about pollution? We can't expect the private sector to keep the air and water clean."

Don unclasped his hands, displaying his open, empty palms. "Sure, air and water pollution potentially harms everyone. This is the legitimate role of government, to protect us against harm. Without laws against pollution, a company might have an incentive to pollute because the potential harm to the company would be small compared to the potential economic gains from polluting. So we need to have laws against pollution, reasonable laws."

Lorna unfolded her arms and looked Don in the eye. "It's convincing when you say it, Don. It makes sense in my head, but I don't feel it in my gut."

Don shifted his right knee on the couch, turning to face her and look her in the eye. "I have doubts too, at least when I'm not at the diner. But doubts shouldn't stop people from trying, from experimenting. That's how America started, and that's why secession is important. Maybe FND is wrong about what will work, but we need the laboratory space to find out if we're wrong. In the meantime, let the SVR try a different experiment in their laboratory in Vermont."

Lorna frowned. "That would be chaos."

"Maybe. But I'd prefer chaos to what we have now. The federalism of the United States was supposed to allow each state to be its own experiment in democracy, but through the years the power and autonomy of the states has disappeared. We have one central government, and those of us who don't like it and don't see a better alternative in any other nation are stuck, unless we secede."

"That's too extreme, Don. The whole scenario seems more like something for a movie than something that could really happen."

"That's what I thought, but Mackey says that in another year we'll have five hundred thousand votes for secession—that's all we need."

"Things never work out the way you plan, Don."

"Mackey knows. He says the battle plan never survives the first shot; it's improvisation from there."

Lorna stood up. "But, Don, let's say that the plans can be improvised and things can be made to work. Isn't Mackey being a little naive in thinking that the United States is just going to let North Dakota secede? And what about the natives? Even if you have a majority vote in favor of secession, isn't it unfair to the natives who don't want to secede?"

Don stood up to meet her gaze. "The natives would be free to move to any of the 49 states. Hell, if the SVR secedes too then there would be that option in Vermont as well—and maybe the secessions will inspire others. More options. How many ways can you get your coffee at Starbucks? But when it comes to government you're stuck with Democrats or Republicans, the difference between which is no more than the difference between Skippy and Jif peanut butter."

"Sure, my business is all about options. Aside from saps like you," Lorna said, poking Don in the chest, "who become monogamous with their girls, most guys want to choose from the menu, enjoy the spice of life."

"Exactly."

"But, Don, telling the natives they're free to pick up and move to another state isn't like telling people they're free to order their mocha latte as decaf or regular. There's a major upheaval in leaving the land that your family has lived on and called home for generations. These people didn't do anything wrong to deserve to be uprooted."

"What about you? You left your family in Virginia, came to New York, and now here you are in North Dakota."

"Hey, I'm here to visit you, not start a revolution. Besides, I'm different."

Don sat down, but the springs in the old couch wouldn't let him find a comfortable position. "This is not a perfect solution, Lorna. But the plan is to accommodate the natives who don't want to secede, to let them keep their United States citizenship. They'll be like Americans living and working in Canada."

Lorna turned her back, walking to the window and saying, "But what about the federal government? Assuming they don't stop you from putting the vote for secession on the ballot, what makes you think they'll let you secede?"

Don shifted on the couch, saying, "We can't win a military war to secede, but the real war is a public-relations war. That's why the feds have been treading so lightly. They could have stepped in to stop or slow things, but they haven't. They haven't wanted to be seen as trampling on freedoms of speech or assembly. But it's only a matter of time before they start with the T word."

Lorna spun around. "Which is?"

"Treason."

# 11

Two weeks into her stay, Lorna had to see it for herself, the New York novelist pouring coffee and wiping the counter at a North Dakota diner. Bells jingled as she walked in the door, and heads turned as she glided across the red-vinyl booth. Mary Mackey took her order, "A garden omelet with Swiss, no toast, no potatoes. Coffee and water."

"Sure thing, sugar. Comin' right up," Mary replied.

Everyone knew who she was—Don's girlfriend was visiting from New York. Who else could it be? Lorna worked her phone and iPad waiting for the food. Things weren't busy, so Mackey cooked on the grill out front. He wasn't cooking bacon but somehow the smell of it filled the air. On the radio Mick Jagger sang about how you can't always get what you want.

Mary came with the coffee. Five minutes later she returned with the food, saying, "Here ya go, sugar."

"That was fast."

Mary winked, saying, "That's how they do it in New York, isn't it?"

"Is it that obvious?"

"Just not so hard to figure, that's all."

Lorna smiled with her eyes.

"You want anything else right now? Some more coffee?"

"Yes please, and some Tabasco."

Mary grabbed the Tabasco and gestured at Don to refill Lorna's cup. Don topped her off and made his rounds, warming cups across the diner.

Don had never mentioned the food. Mackey's Diner was a hub of FND activity and ongoing conversation, so Lorna had assumed the food was just an excuse to gather. At first she couldn't determine what made the omelet so delicious. It wasn't fluffy, so that was good, and she actually didn't need the Tabasco to tame the egg taste. But there was something more. It was the onions. They were fried. Not just sautéed a bit, but fried, practically burned. That's where the flavor came from.

Lorna looked at her phone and eavesdropped on a conversation in the next booth. A round man in green overalls with a long salt-and-pepper beard was speaking. "There's plenty of things people don't want and wouldn't want unless they saw someone else with 'em. Then they don't just want what the other person has. They demand it."

His skinny colleague wearing a red and black flannel shirt put down his coffee and asked, "Whaddya mean?"

"Like figgy pudding."

"What the hell is figgy pudding?"

"You know, from the Christmas song."

"Who the hell likes figgy pudding?"

"That's my point. At Christmas times in the olden days, roles were reversed. Servants and peasants came into the homes of their masters and demanded the best food and drink. Regular people didn't like friggin' figgy pudding, but they saw rich people eatin' it and they barged into the mansion and demanded it."

"Really?"

"You betcha. People see you got some figgy pudding and they start demanding some for themselves. There's a lot of that shit around Christmas time. Santa Claus gets reversed, though. He breaks into your house, but he's not there to take your stuff. He's there to give you stuff!"

"Like figgy pudding?"

"Don't be stupid. You know what I mean. And think of the Christmas tips we're expected to give some people. It's a safety valve."

"Safety from what?"

"Envy. It builds up, and you have to let off steam. That's the way the welfare system works. We don't want people breaking into our houses to take what they want. So we just give 'em what they want from the hand of government. We buy off bad behavior."

"But that don't work with kids."

"Exactly, and it don't work with adults neither. Kids want more and more. So do adults. Kids get to feelin' entitled to it. So do adults."

From behind, Lorna heard Mary's voice asking, "Anything else now?"

Lorna jumped slightly in her seat.

"Sorry, didn't mean to scare you."

"No, that's all right. Just the check, thanks."

Lorna felt like she had been caught peering through a keyhole.

Mary returned with the check and said, "Nice to meet you, miss."

"Lorna, call me Lorna."

"Hope to see you again soon, Lorna."

Lorna put away her phone and iPad before slipping into her black leather jacket. She winked at Don as he was refilling a customer's cup at the far end of the counter. At the register, Mackey asked, "How was your food?"

"Very good, love the fried onions."

"That's my secret. Not much of a secret, actually. I add 'em to just about everything."

"Most places don't take the time to fry them."

"That's right. Glad you liked them."

Mackey was taller than she expected, and he seemed to lean to one side. His face was weathered, but his brown eyes were keen. Lorna paid the check with her American Express card and then walked back to the table to leave a five-dollar bill for a tip. When she turned to look for Don, she saw only Mackey standing behind the counter. He nodded.

* * *

"You're a little piggly wiggly, aren't you?"

"Yes, mistress."

She flicked her raven mane and fixed him with her dark eyes, "Big old federal agent, snooping around Fargo, but you're really just a baby piggy, aren't you?"

"Yes, mistress."

"How pathetic. Here, put this snout on and roll around for me."

"Yes, mistress."

"Now, what does a little piggy say?"

"Oink, oink."

"I can't hear you."

"Oink, oink."

"Very good. For that you get a prize."

She pinned a curly tail on his bare bottom.

"Ooh, ouch."

"Little piggies don't say ouch, do they?"

"No, mistress."

"What do they say?"

"I don't know."

"They squeal. Let me here you squeal."

At the end of the hour Webster Daniels dressed and handed her two one-hundred-dollar bills.

"You know I don't take this shit," she said.

"I can't pay you in goldens," Daniels said.

"You can and you will."

"Yes, mistress."

* * *

"A prostitute, Andy? Do we really have to associate with a

prostitute?"

"She's not a prostitute, Sally. She's a madam."

"But she used to be a prostitute, right? And now she just pimps out other women?"

"Yes, she used to be a prostitute, and yes she arranges things for other women. But try not to judge her in advance. There's something about her."

"Oh God, so you have a crush on this whore?"

"No, you'll see. Anyway, you remember Don, right? You met him when he visited Vermont. He's a writer, or he used to be. Maybe you've even read one of his books, *Body of Evidence*? Anyway, she's just visiting him."

"If I tug on my left ear, Andy, you know what that means."

"I know. It's time to go."

"That's right. We make an excuse and we leave early."

The following evening the couples met at Reginald's in Fargo. The décor hadn't changed since the '70s, and people pretended it had stayed the same on purpose. The Johnsons arrived first and were seated by the maître d'.

"Of course they're late," Sally said.

"They'll be here soon."

"Oh sure, she probably just had a last-minute date to arrange."

"Be nice."

Five minutes later, the maître d' led Don and Lorna to the table. Andy and Sally rose. The men shook hands and made the introductions. Too soon, the waiter appeared soliciting drink orders from Don and Lorna. Andy already had a draft beer in front of him, and Sally was sipping a cosmopolitan.

"I'll have a diet Coke," Lorna said.

"I'll have a Bud draft," Don added.

"How are things at the diner?" Andy asked.

"Fine. But we haven't seen you in a few days."

"Just busy with work, been meaning to stop in."

"So have you been able to keep your old clients from Vermont?"

"Some of them, but the move cost me most of them."

The men drifted into conversation about the North Dakota State football team, which had won the Division I AA national championship again.

"More exciting than anything we got in Vermont," Andy said.

"New York too. No good college football in New York, definitely not in the city. Syracuse upstate, but they're more basketball."

Don lamented that he never had a son to watch football with. Don's daughter had given him grandchildren, but Don had no hope that they would watch football with him either. They were unathletic and coddled. "You have to let kids make mistakes and get hurt. I can't help but imagine a sickly generation of adults coming from this generation of kids. They'll have no tolerance for pain, hurt, loss, disappointment, and setback. Those are the kinds of experiences kids need to grow strong."

"That's what Andy says, too," Sally said. "I was a wreck when our Michael fell out of a tree and broke his arm, but Andy broke his arm when he was a kid. So he had a different way of looking at it."

"Yeah, it's a vivid memory for me," Andy said. "I missed the second half of the little-league season when I was 12, and so I didn't get to even try out for the travel team. I liked the attention that came with wearing the cast and having all my friends sign it. And the time it took to get the cast off seemed to be forever. But it was a touchstone for me. Whenever I had a setback, I could think about the broken arm. Not only had my body healed, but I got over the disappointment of not getting to play on the travel team. It gave me a confidence that other kids didn't have."

"What about you, Lorna?" asked Sally.

"I've had it pretty easy, never broke a bone."

"Really?"

"Sure, life has been good. I mean sure, there have been disappointments. My Uncle Dave went to prison for fraud when I was about fourteen. I had a hard time making sense of the fact that the man who was so good to me had hurt other people. People aren't always what they seem."

"That's it? That was your big disappointment?"

"Well, that was the most dramatic one. I never really knew my mother. She died in a car crash when I was a baby. My father drifted away slowly. He's pretty religious, didn't want me to go to college in New York. By the time I dropped out of law school, he was mostly just praying for me, not talking to me."

"That's so sad."

"My decisions haven't seemed right to him, but I wouldn't have felt right if I just did what he wanted me to."

"But I mean too about your mother, that you never knew her."

Lorna sat back and looked away, saying, "I guess you don't miss what you never had."

"You work with what you have," Don said, with empty hands turned upward.

"I know about that," Sally said. "Everyone thought we were out of our minds when we decided to leave Vermont. But all the pieces have been fitting together. It feels right."

"Like *Tetris*," Lorna said.

"Like what?"

"Like *Tetris*. You make all the pieces fit, and it feels good."

Sally smiled and said, "That kind of makes sense. Don't take this the wrong way, but you're not quite what I expected."

"That's all right. Neither are you." Lorna displayed her perfect white teeth, but the smile came from her eyes.

On the drive home, Andy said, "I'm sorry if I missed it when you tugged your ear."

"Shut up," Sally said. "You know I didn't tug my ear."

"So they're all right?"

"I don't know about Don, but Lorna, yeah. She's gonna watch the kids when I go to the dentist Friday."

\* \* \*

Fritz Muller and his roommate Bobby Blanchard thought they were being ignored. No one took their order. But ten minutes later Mackey came over with a huge platter of fries covered with nacho cheese and ground beef. "I'll bring you a couple of Cokes," was all he said. Since that time they had been back again and again with a growing group of friends. Fritz wore flip flops even in winter and Bobby had white-man's dreadlocks. The others weren't quite as obvious, but they were all stoners. On their second visit to the diner, Fritz and Bobby overheard Mackey discussing drug legalization with a guy at the counter.

"This guy is the coolest," Bobby said.

"Yeah, he's like Gandalf," Fritz said.

"No, dude, he's like Obi Wan Kenobi."

The boys made a habit of just eating their fries and listening to Mackey and his customers. Then on the drive back to North Dakota State, they'd dissect what they heard. Most of the talk had to do with economics, but it all had to do with liberty, freedom. Mackey had no patience for blaming other people or blaming society. That was a new idea for Fritz, complete freedom with complete responsibility. No excuses.

At the diner one stoned Saturday afternoon, there wasn't much to listen to, and so Fritz started spouting off about how most of the founding fathers grew hemp and that's why the pursuit of happiness is guaranteed in the Declaration of Independence. Don had no one to pour coffee for, so he took the opportunity to remind the boys that the basic ideas go back to John Locke, who had written about the right to private property, not the pursuit of happiness.

"Yeah, but that's obvious," Fritz said, stroking his orange beard.

"If it's so obvious, then why does the government take my private property without my permission?" Don replied.

"They don't, they can't."

"What about income taxes?"

"That's just the money the government needs to run."

"Did you know that income taxes were prohibited by the original version of the Constitution?"

"That can't be right."

"Look it up. It wasn't until the 16th Amendment in 1913 that we got a permanent income tax."

Bobby checked his phone and joined in, "He's right, dude. It's on Wikipedia."

Don continued, "At first it was just a low tax on the very wealthy, but guess what happened? Government power grew gradually. Now, top earners can pay nearly 50% of their income in taxes."

"Whoa."

"That's right, 'whoa.' Along with life and liberty, property is one of the three main things that Locke saw government as protecting. But instead of protecting, now it's taking."

Inspired by his conversation with the stoners, Don began to blog. *"The threat of force is concealed in laws. If you smoke pot, you fail to comply with the law. If you are caught, you will be fined. And if you fail to pay the fine, men will come to your house with guns. You will be jailed. Your freedom will be taken away by force. Don't pay your taxes and your freedom will be taken away by force. Tax laws have the illusion of legitimacy, but in fact they are voted for by people who stand to benefit at the cost of those who stand to lose. When the income tax was enacted in 1913 it placed only a light burden on the very wealthy. They should have stood up and cried foul, but the sacrifice was so small that they would have appeared greedy and selfish. Today the tax rate on upper-income earners is nearly 50%, and the percentage of the population who pay income taxes has gone from 1% to 53%. This trend is destined to continue as long as the majority of people derive more benefits from the income tax than they actually pay in taxes. It would be easier to protest if taxes weren't taken right out of your paycheck. In fact, income-tax compliance rates soared during World War II when the government started taking taxes out of every paycheck rather than leaving it to individuals to pay their taxes by April 15. Of course, most self-employed people and independent business owners don't have paychecks. Instead, they are bound by law to estimate their own tax bill and pay it four times a year. They should stop doing so or move to North Dakota."*

Lorna was lying on her back in the living room reading the blog on her iPad. She laughed, saying, "So you blame people for paying taxes? No wonder you love me. It's hard to pay taxes when you run an illegal business."

Don was in the kitchen mixing his Metamucil. Tossing his spoon in the sink, he said, "I don't blame the people as much as I blame the politicians. They want to give people more to make them dependent. People start off wanting to fend for themselves, hesitant to take a handout."

Lorna put down the iPad. "Come on, Don," she said. "People will take whatever is being given."

Don gulped some of his Metamucil. "I don't think so. Sure, under the worst circumstances they'll take help from friends or family, or maybe even from neighbors or the church. But they don't want money seized from fellow citizens."

"Yeah, but they don't see it that way, Don."

"Of course not. They think the money comes from a rich government with coffers overflowing, like the Queen of England with her crown jewels. Or they think the government just plays

Robin Hood by taking the money from rich people who prey on the poor. The first generation to take the money did it with an uneasy conscience, but the politicians told them they were entitled to it. Everyone knew it was a lie."

Lorna sat up on the floor. "So why don't people today know it's a lie?"

"Think of the Garden of Eden. The generation that produced the story didn't think it was literally true, but later generations did. Or think of George Washington chopping down a cherry tree and Paul Revere single-handedly spreading the word that 'The British are coming!'"

"OK, so?"

"So over time stories are presumed true. Most people don't consider who pays for their benefits; it's as if they magically appear. And those who do think about it conclude that they're paid for by people who have done wrong getting rich in the first place."

Lorna raised an eyebrow and said, "Maybe. But one thing's for sure."

"What?"

"You have to keep stirring that Metamucil."

Don looked at the nearly solid orange mass in the glass and walked back into the kitchen for a spoon.

# 12

Sally was treating Lorna to lunch at Panera near the university, a "thank you" for watching the kids. They sat in the middle of the place at the only table available, surrounded by chattering white people.

"You've ruined Michael and Lisa for me," Sally said.

"Oh no," Lorna said, widening her eyes and leaning back. "What do you mean?"

"They're going to want the crusts taken off their peanut-butter-and-jelly sandwiches from now on."

"Hah. You scared me," she said, exhaling loudly.

"Sorry about that."

"Well you better not bring them here. All these soups, and salads, and breads, and panini."

"Actually, I have brought the kids here. They hated it. I had to drive through McDonald's on the way home."

"Well, kids have their own sense of taste. Arts and crafts and peanut butter and jelly, right?" Lorna forked her turkey Cobb salad.

"Yeah, that's right. It's everything, though. Food, activities, music, TV, movies, clothes. By the way, what's that song you taught them? Lisa keeps singing it?"

"Which one?"

"The one about the sun and the moon and the stars." Sally took a bite of her portabella and provolone panini.

"Oh that was just a silly little tune we made up together." Before Sally could respond, Lorna continued, "So how was the dentist?"

Sally swept her tongue around her mouth and then smiled with her newly whitened teeth. "What do you think?"

"Lovely, they did a great job. Who's your dentist?"

"Dr. Grossman. I can get you an appointment if you'd like."

"Thanks, but I'll be back in New York before I need a whitening." Lorna looked down at her salad and poked around for an elusive bit of bacon. In truth, Lorna didn't whiten her teeth.

"So you're heading back soon?"

"Yeah, I've been running the business by phone and computer, but I can't keep doing that forever. Besides, it's cold as hell here."

Sally laughed. "Yeah, I thought I would mind the cold more, but the sun is so bright that it makes up for it." It was true. In Vermont, Sally rarely left the house in winter, but in North Dakota, she had become a daily walker and now a runner.

"I love your nails. Now that's something I can't put off until I get back to New York. Where do you get them done?"

Sally blushed. "There's a great place near my house, the Woodsbridge Spa. Well, it's not really a spa. But they do a really nice mani-pedi. Maybe we could go together sometime?"

"How about next Wednesday?"

"It's a date."


At the apartment Don was getting dressed for a shift at the diner when Lorna returned. His *Tetris* game and Metamucil were on the coffee table.

"How was your lunch?" Don asked from the bedroom.

"Very nice. She's a sweetie."

"I'm still surprised she likes you."

"What's not to like?"

"Hey, I agree."

"Can you put away your game and your poop medicine before you go?"

"This is my place."

"Sorry, you're right."

Don walked into the living room and cleared off the coffee table.

"I told her I liked her nails. I really did, actually."

"No wonder she likes you."

"What do you mean?"

"That's like having Einstein tell you he likes your equation."

Lorna had a story to tell about herself every day. She could frame the day's narrative, but she couldn't put it in the context of her life's narrative. What did today's story about lunch with Sally have to do with the past? And where was it leading her? Don's theory was that we don't tell stories about ourselves to imitate stories we've heard. Instead, we tell stories in books and movies because we naturally tell stories about ourselves. Our way of understanding ourselves is to see ourselves as part of a narrative with a beginning, middle, and end. We're constantly understanding ourselves in terms of a past that we revise and rationalize and a future that we predict and anticipate. That's the structure our minds naturally impose on our reality, and so it's no wonder that we tell stories about other people for the purposes of entertainment and education.

\* \* \*

Lorna let her long fingers walk through the menu. She had started sitting at the counter during her visits to the diner. Of course she knew what she wanted, but she still liked to peruse the menu. Mackey took her order, "Garden omelet with Swiss cheese, no potatoes, no toast. Coffee and water."

Mackey nodded with eyes closed and a half-smile as if to say "excellent choice." He gave the order to Sam in the kitchen and came back with the coffee.

"Thanks. Why do you do so much of the work here yourself, Mackey? Why don't you just sit back and collect the money?"

"Because I enjoy the work. There's a pleasure in serving others."

"I get that."

"Then you probably also get that there's no pleasure in being made to serve others involuntarily."

"Uh-oh, where's this going, Mackey? I just came for some fried onions in my omelet."

"Sorry. Mary will be right out with your order." Mackey turned and began to wipe down the coffee maker.

"Ah, don't do that. You know I was just playing hard to get."

Mackey turned with raised eyebrows.

Lorna continued, "No one likes to be forced to serve, I get that. But don't you need to give people illusions?"

"If people pay for an illusion, that's fine—that's what going to the movies is for. But when you're not paying for something it's charity. There's nothing wrong with taking charity as long as you don't kid yourself."

Lorna poured cream in her coffee and stirred it thoughtfully. "But isn't there more dignity in accepting help from the government than from charity? Isn't that why we do it that way? People are too proud to accept help from charities, and by the time they're desperate enough to accept charity, they're so broken that their last shred of dignity is a cruel price to demand."

"Yes, but…"

Swallowing some coffee, Lorna bulged her eyes at Mackey. "But what?"

He continued, "But the important thing is to give people the help they need. That calls for humane, compassionate distribution. Some private charities have been heavy-handed in the past, especially religiously-based charities that made people feel like sinners. I saw it myself when I worked with the homeless."

"So, I'm right, then, Mackey?"

Mary brought the omelet. Lorna cut in right away and put a piece in her mouth. Most places put the cheese on too soon, and it liquefied, losing its taste and texture. Not Mackey's. The cheese was melted just right when you got the omelet hot off the grill.

"Not completely," Mackey replied. "We need to acknowledge

our benefactors as benefactors. We can't simply take from them and pretend we haven't done so. Honesty has to cut both ways. Government confiscation and redistribution of wealth, no matter how well intended, obscures the truth that the charity has come from fellow citizens. And, even worse, it depicts the government itself as the benefactor."

Lorna took another bite of her omelet, savoring the taste of the fried onions blending with the cheese. The egg was thin and its taste subtle, nearly imperceptible, a surface on which other flavors were painted. "I like an honest approach, but you can't hit someone over the head with what you've done for them," she said.

Mackey nodded. "You're right, Lorna, but the welfare state has gone too far in the other direction. Not only do they not make people feel badly about accepting charity, they make people feel like they are owed what they are getting, that it's an entitlement, not charity."

Lorna gritted her teeth and then bit her tongue gently before replying. "I know all about the dance of pretense. A whore takes your money but then acts like she's giving it to you for free. The pretense is what you're paying for, though, and so there's a deeper honesty to it."

Don refilled her coffee without a word as he made his rounds.

Lorna continued, "So, OK, it's charity, Mackey. I get that. But isn't it just simpler to have a law that funds charity rather than count on people to give voluntarily to charity?"

Mackey bent over, resting his fists and forearms on the counter. "A law can seem like a good solution to just about any problem. But people don't foresee the unintended consequences of the laws they want."

Lorna took her last bite of the omelet and squinted at Mackey, asking, "What do you mean?"

Mackey stood up straight and folded his arms. "Well, think about the minimum wage. Sounds like a good idea to have a law that specifies a minimum wage, right?"

"Sure, it protects people from being taken advantage of."

Mackey put both hands on the counter and leaned in. "That's what everyone sees, Lorna, but what they don't see is that employers can't afford to pay employees more than what they're worth. So the unintended consequence of the minimum-wage law is that some of the workers the law is meant to benefit will be harmed by having their number of hours cut—and some will actually lose their jobs."

Lorna slumped her shoulders and sipped her coffee. The diner buzzed with conversation and activity, but she had forgotten about it. It was as if Mackey was talking to her from the other end of a tunnel, with the rest of the world outside.

Mackey continued, "It's even harder to see the invisible unintended consequences. Think about the jobs that are never created as a result of minimum-wage laws because an employer can't afford to hire anyone at that level, even though the employer would have been able to hire someone at a lower hourly rate. Thanks to minimum-wage laws there are practically no gas-station attendants pumping gas, even though young men would be willing to do it for less than minimum wage."

Lorna clinked her coffee cup on its saucer. "Still, wouldn't things be even worse for workers without minimum-wage laws?"

Don came over to refill her cup. She had felt him watching from across the diner. What was his problem? Was he jealous?

"Do you know what percentage of the work force is paid the minimum wage, Lorna?"

"I'd guess about 20%."

"It's 5%. For 95% of workers, employers don't need to be told to pay more than the minimum wage. At least they don't need the government to tell them. The market tells them. They know that if they don't pay employees what they're worth those employees will leave to work somewhere else. That's how the free market works in distributing labor."

Mary cleared her plate and Lorna smiled in acknowledgment before redirecting her gaze to the man at the other end of the tunnel. "Yeah, but Mackey, the minimum wage sets a starting point. Everyone's wage or salary would be lower if there were no minimum wage or if the minimum wage were lower."

"It's tempting to think that, but if it were true, then we should set the minimum wage much higher so that we could increase everyone's income. Why not make it twenty dollars an hour? Or one hundred dollars an hour? That would seemingly raise everyone's income in reaction to the minimum wage. But you can see the problem with that, right?"

Lorna winced. "Yeah, it would lead to massive unemployment because employers couldn't afford to pay the price."

Mackey nodded. "A market will set its own minimum wage for each person. Each person should be free to contract to work for whatever he or she is willing to work for. You know it from your business, right?"

Lorna sighed. "Yeah, on the streets, some women are willing to sell themselves for a hit on a crack pipe, and in the penthouse some women charge six figures." Lorna had heard horror stories about women who got hooked on crack and went from the penthouse to the streets. That elevator only goes down, never up.

"Even though it's illegal," Mackey said, "prostitution is a free market. Prices are determined by buyers and sellers without government interference. How would a government official know the proper price anyway?"

Lorna smirked. "Well, without disclosing any names, I can tell you that a lot of government officials have good firsthand knowledge of the market."

"Funny. But you take my point. The balance of supply and demand sets the price more effectively than a bureaucrat could. Government involvement obscures things. Think about what happens when someone gets a welfare check from the government rather than help from a private charity or benefits from an insurance claim. The amount may be the same, but the effect is different."

Lorna looked left in response to the sound of a broken glass. Renata was stooping to address the mess. "How do you mean?" Lorna asked.

"The financial incentive to find work is diminished. If you can collect a welfare check that allows you a minimal standard of living, why would you take a job that pays a low wage that will not improve your standard of living?"

"You'd take the job, Mackey, because it feels good to make your own money. Right?"

"Maybe. Certainly if you felt like you were doing something wrong by not taking the job. And you would feel that way if you were taking money from family and friends while you were out of work."

Don came by, raising the coffee pot with a nonverbal offer to refill. She looked at her cup and seeing it more than half full waved him off before replying to Mackey, "But not if you're taking money from the government?"

Mackey waved to a departing customer before resuming his tunnel vision. "Not as likely, Lorna, because you think the government has lots of money and you've paid into the system. And even if you're aware that the government doesn't really have any money, that it just takes money from other people who pay into the system and spreads it around, you probably think those other people have done things wrong and owe it to you."

Lorna sipped her coffee, which was growing cold. She should have taken a warm up from Don. "Yeah, but isn't welfare like an insurance plan? We all pay in, and so when we have the bad luck to lose our job we collect on the insurance."

"That's right, Lorna. But it's a government-run insurance plan, which means that it's much less efficient than a private insurance plan. If you had private unemployment insurance, you can bet the insurance agents would be placing you in a job quickly, and if you turned down the job then that would nullify your policy. No more benefits."

"Harsh," she said draining her cup.

"A little, but it wouldn't have to be. Before the rise of the welfare state, there were mutual-aid societies that people paid into like insurance plans. Most of them were local or ethnic-centered groups, and they were administered with compassion and fairness."

Lorna crossed her arms. "So that's your plan? Mutual-aid societies?"

"They'd be an option, but larger private insurance companies would probably do a better job. Predicting the future is a fool's game. We won't know what works best in the future until the future is the present." Mackey shrugged, turned, and pushed through the doors into the kitchen.

Lorna turned and caught sight of Don averting his eyes. What was his problem?

# 13

When Ben first met Sarah at the hospital, he had to look away, but then he found his eyes lingering.

"Oh, do I have something on my cheek?" Sarah asked. "Must be the spaghetti sauce from lunch."

"No, no," Ben said. "Sorry, was I staring? That's a bad habit of mine when I meet somebody new." He extended his hand. "Ben Andersen."

"Yes, Dr. Andersen, I know who you are. I'm Sarah Jurgensen, the new nurse, obviously," she said, waving at her uniform and ID badge.

"Nice to meet you, Sarah." Ben dared to look straight at her, and she held his gaze for a beat before they parted.

Sarah had done ROTC to pay for college, and she was now a lieutenant in the Army Reserve. During her four years of active duty after college, Sarah had been harassed repeatedly. It didn't matter how unattractive she looked in her uniform. Some guys seemed to take it as a challenge. Assuming she was a lesbian, they'd start in with the carpet-munching innuendo and end up suggesting they had what she really needed. To these guys a pure lesbian seemed an impossibility—a woman needed a dick. There had been unwelcome touching and groping, but taking it up the chain of command would only have made matters worse. Civilian life suited Sarah better.

Ben was still smarting from the loss of Brittney when Sarah started at United. The other doctors joked about getting her a smaller nose and bigger breasts for the Secret Santa exchange. Ben laughed along, but for months he thought that some guy would be lucky to have her. Cops liked nurses, but none of them would go for her. Maybe some librarian or professor or scientist.

Despite himself, Ben continued to stare as if her face were a car wreck. After the first time, Sarah ceased asking if she had something on her cheek. Most men didn't notice her at all, and those who did were confused. Like a little boy who gets caught playing with a doll, they would quickly distance themselves with a slur. Late one Wednesday afternoon, Sarah sat alone at a table in the back of the cafeteria near the vending machines. The fluorescent lights overhead buzzed and flickered. When Ben spotted her from a distance she held up a Granny Smith. "Damn," she said as he approached.

"What's the matter?"

"I thought these things were like garlic to you guys. An apple a day keeps the doctor away. You know, like garlic and vampires."

"Ah, you got me. Sorry, I'll leave you alone."

"Just kidding." Sarah tilted her head as she stretched towards him. "Want a bite?"

"What? Your neck?"

"No, I gave blood yesterday. Want a bite of the apple?"

"The apple? Is there a talking snake around here?"

"I didn't see any, but I can't rule it out."

Ben bit the apple. "I'll take my chances."

During her first semester of college Sarah had been the prize winner for an ugly-date contest. The men of Alpha Epsilon Theta had a tradition of "going pigging" for the first fall dance. Everyone threw in a hundred bucks, and the guy who brought the ugliest girl to the dance took the pot. It was a well-known tradition on campus, and so girls steered clear.

Sarah had noticed Chuck Kolbeck staring at her in biology lab, and so when he asked her to the AET fall dance she gushed. It wasn't until a week after the dance that she understood. Chuck took her home early that night, saying that he had to study, but he kissed her gently outside her dorm. When he ignored her in lab and didn't call, Sarah told her roommate Jessica.

"Oh. My. God," Jessica said. "He's AET? And you went to the dance?"

"Yeah, and we had such a nice time, I thought. I guess I should just forget about it."

"Sweetie, that's what you have to do. Forget about it and don't tell anyone."

"Why shouldn't I tell anyone?"

"Just don't. Let's keep it between us."

But Sarah couldn't forget it. She recalled Janelle from her floor saying "congratulations" with a smirk the day after the dance. Two days after the conversation with her roommate, Sarah saw Janelle and her friend Cindy sitting on the blue foam cushioned couch in the dorm lounge. Over the blare of the TV Sarah asked, "What did you mean when you said 'congratulations' the day after the dance?" Janelle laughed. Her friend Cindy widened her eyes in surprise and covered her mouth with her hand.

"You really don't know?" Janelle said with a forced laugh.

"Don't know what?"

"You won the prize?"

"No I didn't... What prize?"

"Did you notice anything about the other girls at the dance?"

"No, not really."

Janelle giggled. "O-K-aay. Did you notice that Cindy and I weren't there even though our boyfriends are in AET?"

Sarah shrugged.

"You won the blue ribbon, the pig prize. And really, that's amazing, because you're not even fat. Strom Ulrich brought a 300-pound heifer and you beat her. So yeah, con-grat-u-lations."

Tears streamed silently down Sarah's face before she could turn to leave. Shielding her eyes, she stared down at the gray concrete steps as she shuffled up three flights. After fumbling with her keys and collapsing face down on her bed, Sarah sobbed into the pillow until she fell asleep.

Ben had pledged AET and been rejected. He hated those kinds of guys, at least that's what he told himself. Actually, he worked hard in college to get into med school to become a doctor to drive the kind of cars those guys drove and to screw the kind of girls those guys screwed. All his hard work paid off with Brittney and a BMW. Ben had misgivings, not just about Brittney, but about his career. He enjoyed the automatic respect that came with being a doctor, but the hours were long and the work was dull. It was a job.

When Sarah offered him a bite of her apple things changed. With her large nose and sunken chin, Sarah was hard to look at in certain lights. Mousey brown hair did nothing to frame her face, but when she smiled it would spread to her big brown eyes with a twinkle. Up close, he smelled her sweet breath and noticed a heart-shaped mole on her neck. After taking a small bite from the Granny Smith, he put it back on the table. Sarah raised her eyebrows in response.

"What?" he asked.

"How did it taste?

"Fine, why?"

"Because there's half a worm left sticking out of the apple."

Startled, Ben looked at the apple and then at Sarah.

"Gotcha."

Ben kicked back in his chair. "Yeah, you got me. You got me."

In that moment her nose became perfect. You couldn't block it out, and you couldn't look past it. Her brown eyes weren't easy to fix upon. They weren't just there for the taking. You had to get past the nose, but once you did, you could see the sparkle and you could sense the symmetry that gave order to her imperfections.

"How about getting coffee?" Ben asked.

"I have coffee," she said, pointing to the blue and orange striped Styrofoam cup.

"Some other time? Or dinner, away from this place?"

"Is this some kind of joke?"

"No, I'm sorry if I'm bothering you. I usually don't date nurses."

"You prefer yoga instructors? Models? Strippers?"

"No, I just mean I don't usually date people from work."

"Do you do Secret Santa? Because I heard some of the docs had really clever ideas for what to get me."

"Those guys are assholes, overgrown frat boys. I'm sorry."

"I'll think about it."

"OK, no pressure. I'll leave you with your apple."

# 14

Lorna sat at the counter sipping coffee after her lunch, a buffalo burger. Bison steak was too lean for her taste, but the burgers were just fatty enough to be flavorful. Mackey presented the burger on a Kaiser roll with lettuce and tomato, accompanied by his signature fresh-cut fries. Lorna pretended to check text messages while eavesdropping on Don as he chatted with some North Dakota State stoners. She looked up to find Mackey standing in front of her.

"How do you do that?" she asked.

"Do what?"

"Just appear. Are you a ninja or something?"

"You just weren't paying attention, too busy listening to your boyfriend."

"It amazes me that he has this whole worldview."

Mackey chuckled.

Lorna put down her phone. "Don't laugh at me."

"Why? Because you didn't say anything funny?"

"That's right." She scowled.

"You're used to men laughing when you say anything you intend to be even slightly humorous, right?"

"Yes, it gets annoying."

"And women aren't much better, right?"

"Right. The girl crushes get old."

"But I'm laughing at you for some reason that you don't understand. And that makes you feel uncomfortable."

"Of course." Her mind wandered. What was the point of this grilling? She felt like she was back in law school.

Mackey leaned against the stainless-steel fridge, trying to keep his back straight. "That's good. It's good to get out of your comfort zone. But here's why I'm laughing. There are millions of people like you who don't think they have a worldview, definitely not a political worldview. And they're the people moving to North Dakota."

"What do you mean?" She looked around the diner, as if a glance would reveal what she had in common with these misfits. Larry Rhinehart had stepped out for a smoke, leaving the newspaper on his stool to save his place at the counter. He drew deeply on his Marlboro and exhaled with an ease that suggested he was in charge, that he had not been driven into the cold involuntarily by an overwhelming craving for nicotine.

"You're an entrepreneur, Lorna."

Lorna crossed her arms. "Yeah, so?" *Oh boy, here it comes,* she thought.

"You were going to be a lawyer, but you saw there was a better way to make money as a prostitute. You went to work for an agency, for a madam?"

"For a guy, actually." The stoners had gone, and roles had reversed. Don was now eavesdropping on Lorna. What was with him? She wondered whether his money troubles were getting to him.

"Fine," Mackey said. "But you were always your own boss in a way, right?"

"Yeah, I was dependent on the guy to set things up and provide protection and collect the money, but I thought of myself as my own boss. I could always go to another agency. This wasn't street-level stuff, no threat of harm."

Mackey waved goodbye to a departing customer, and returned his gaze to Lorna. "So you were free to move from one employer to another?"

"Right, and if I got a bad vibe from a john, I left the gig. And if I didn't like a john I wouldn't see him again." Lorna spied the bacon on the burger Renata was carrying. Bacon on a buffalo burger would be perfect.

"So you always worked for yourself?"

Lorna snapped from her bacon-buffalo-burger fantasy to

reply, "Right, and eventually I had the idea to set up my own agency."

"I bet that wasn't out of the blue. That came out of your worldview, your view that you worked for yourself—you were your own boss."

"That's right." *No, I'm not back in law school,* she mused. *I'm on the witness stand, but no one has told me the charge.*

"And you've been very successful."

Was this the charge, she thought, success? "That's right. Because I treat my employees right and I treat my clients right."

"Some people would say you're just taking advantage of your employees and clients."

Lorna unfolded her arms. "Yeah, but my girls and johns don't say that. No one is forced to work for me and no one has to deal with me. I just do the best job of making it all possible."

"Sounds easy." Mackey gave a nod to a passing customer.

Lorna tilted her head. "Sometimes it is. But I see my competitors messing up all the time."

"So you do have a worldview. You always had one."

Lorna lifted an eyebrow. Don hovered and raised the pot, offering to refill her coffee. She shook her head.

Mackey continued, "You want freedom to exercise your talents and abilities. You value your independence. You value other people and treat them well. But you think of yourself as an individual first. You don't define yourself as a member of a group or a community."

Lorna opened her mouth to speak, but Mackey bulldozed over her, saying, "Sure, you're a member of groups and communities and some of those are important to you. But the individual is more important than the group. Does that all sound right?"

Lorna smirked. "Yeah, but everyone thinks that way. That's like a horoscope—it would fit anyone."

"No, Lorna, that description doesn't fit most people. It fits the people we're trying to reach. They're the people moving to North

Dakota. Like you, most of them don't even realize they have a worldview and that not everyone shares it."

"But what about family, Mackey? That's a group?"

"Right. We need to feel connected to other people. Family members are usually the first to provide those connections, and ideally those connections last. The problem comes when a person thinks of himself first and foremost as a member of a family, and only second as an individual."

Lorna tilted her head to the side and closed her eyes. "That's how it is with my business," she said. "I never call it a family. But some of the girls call me Mom or Sis." Actually, she liked being called Mom. She liked taking care of the girls, looking out for them, giving them the benefit of her experience.

"You never insist on their loyalty or allegiance, though, right?"

"Of course not. They're free to quit the life, or work for someone else, or go out on their own at any time."

"That's what a family does at its best, Lorna. It provides a safe home base. People need to go out into the world as individuals, but they also need a safe home base to come back to."

"If family is so important, how come you never had any children?" Mackey closed his eyes, and Lorna immediately regretted asking the question. "Sorry, that was too personal," she said.

"That's OK. It wasn't in the cards, that's all."

Lorna averted her gaze, pretending to watch Don watching her at the other end of the counter. She had to admit that in a way she was taking care of Don, mothering him. "My father controlled everything. What I ate, what I watched on TV, who I played with, how I dressed. You name it. And all the God stuff, just seemed like so much bullshit after awhile."

Mackey smiled.

"Sorry, no offense."

"None taken, Lorna. I don't much care for people who shove

God down other people's throats. You never hear me mention God, do you?"

Lorna pouted her lower lip and half-nodded. She knew that politics was always on the menu at Mackey's Diner, but not religion. Of course, lots of customers liked to mix the two, but Mackey always managed to move any discussion away from religion.

Mackey continued, "We need to belong; we need to have a home base. But we need to be accepted at home for the ways we differ there."

"That's what Don does. He lets me be who I am. He listens and doesn't try to solve my problems and issues. My father always tried to arrange my life so that there would be no problems. But that's impossible. And when there were problems he provided neat and tidy solutions to them. But Don listens and he doesn't impose solutions. He just lets me be me." Lorna smiled.

Mackey nodded with eyes closed. "You're lucky to have found one another."

"Well, I'm lucky. I don't know what he gets out of it aside from a young body in bed."

"You're not serious."

Lorna shook the bracelets on her left wrist, saying, "I don't know."

"Lorna, most men his age are focused on their legacy. They've done their best work and raised their children and they're just sentimentally concerned with affirming for themselves that they've done some good, left the world a better place than they found it. But Don is doing something new. He doesn't feel like the most important things he's done are in the past."

"I'm not sure about that. He says he can't write anymore. He's blocked up, can't get it out. Besides that, he's nearly broke, and his ex-wife is threatening to sue him for the alimony he owes. Most people think he's crazy."

"But you don't. You've nurtured him. "

"I'm not sure about that."

Mackey raised a skeptical eyebrow.

"Let's get back to the entrepreneur thing," she said.

Don had heard his name and barely concealed his eavesdropping. This time Lorna accepted his offer of a refill, but sensing that the conversation was moving on, Don fetched the giant travel mug he kept under the counter and refilled it with Coke.

"Yes, I always thought of myself as my own boss," Lorna said, "even when I was working for someone else. But not everyone can be their own boss. The world doesn't work that way. Not everyone can be the CEO of their own business. We need some people to work for other people."

"That's right. But it's the state of mind that counts, Lorna. When someone sees himself as potentially working for himself, he's inspired to look for new and better ways of doing things. That's what you did."

She smiled.

Mackey continued, "Competition is good. So sometimes it's actually good when an employee leaves and sets up a competing business. It's good for customers because they have more options and potentially lower prices. And it's good for the business because competition makes us work harder to serve customers better, and it can lead to greater success."

Without a pause, Lorna added, "Plus it avoids a monopoly."

"Right, but be careful about that. There's nothing necessarily bad about a monopoly if it's justly attained and maintained."

"So everything bad is good? Is that what you're saying, Mackey?"

"Not exactly. Government monopolies and government-granted monopolies like the post office and the phone company in the days of yore were bad because they had no incentive to serve their customers well. But a privately held and run monopoly is not guaranteed to remain a monopoly and so it still has to serve its customers well to keep competition at bay."

Lorna looked unconvinced.

"Have you ever heard of A&P?" Mackey asked.

"Sure, the old supermarket chain."

"Actually, they're still around."

"Really? The ones I knew are all closed. There was one right across the street from the house where I grew up. I can still remember the smell, especially in the produce section. It was like no one had ever opened a window and the smell of every fruit and vegetable blended in a nauseating aroma. No wonder that store closed."

"Right, well over 90% of the original stores are closed. But A&P was considered a monopoly at one point, and the government almost stepped in to break up the company."

"What happened?"

"A&P got too comfortable. Smaller competitors came along who offered customers greater variety and higher-quality products and better service. But A&P was too self-satisfied and too stuck in its ways. They didn't innovate. So they went from being a virtual monopoly to being virtually extinct."

Lorna looked down at her coffee as she stirred it. Clinking the spoon on the saucer, she said, "So no monopoly-busting? The government should just stick to regulating industries?"

"Not even that, Lorna. The government's role is to protect us from force, fraud, and theft. So if a company sells us a harmful product or misrepresents its product, that's the place for government intervention. The rule of law needs to be in place and respected. But regulation is a form of pre-punishment. Regulations are there to keep businesses from even coming near to harming people."

Lorna folded her arms. "What's wrong with that? Preventing harm is better than making someone pay for the harm they committed."

"Lorna, think about what has to go into the prevention of harm. It's the restriction of freedom. Anyone who sells tainted meat should be punished, but telling a company what they have to do to ensure that they are not selling tainted meat restricts their freedom."

"That's just stupid, Mackey. You need to prevent harm where you can."

Mary interrupted to ask Lorna if she wanted some dessert, adding "We have pie." Mary Mackey baked the pies herself. Lorna's eyes widened. "You want pecan?" Mary asked.

"Yes, please."

"Warmed up with some whipped cream?"

"You know me well."

Mackey resumed, "Think about it, Lorna. Does the company want to sell tainted meat?"

"Of course not. They'll be punished and they'll probably go out of business because people won't buy meat from them anymore."

"So, do they really need more motivation than that to avoid selling tainted meat?"

"Probably not, but it couldn't hurt."

"Are you sure about that?"

Lorna gazed at the smokers arrayed beyond the diner's steps. "The regulation would prevent harm done by companies and individuals who aren't rational, who don't see that it's in their interest to avoid selling tainted meat."

Mackey nodded. "You're right, Lorna. It might be helpful with unscrupulous and irrational companies and individuals. But you're wrong when you say it couldn't hurt."

"Why is that?"

"Think about this. Who's more likely to know about the proper conditions for producing the product, the company or a government bureaucracy?"

"The company."

"That's right. Regulation often looks good from the outside to people who don't really know the business. But no one likes government regulation in their own business because they know the government is clueless when it comes to the measures they want imposed."

"OK, Mackey, but still, we need some kind of assurance that a product is safe before we buy it."

Mary put the pie in front of her.

"But why should that come from government? Do you ever look at *Consumer Reports* before you buy something?"

"Sure, for computers and electronics," she said.

"*Consumer Reports* does a fine job of testing products and disseminating information, and they are not a government agency. If we did away with government regulation in all industries, we'd see the rise of more private agencies and publications like *Consumer Reports*. And they would keep us safer than we are now. No one would buy meat that wasn't approved by the private organization that investigated and reported on its production."

"Maybe," Lorna said, gently forking a piece of pie. No matter how good it was in her memory, the first taste was better. The warm pecan goo merged with the delicate flaky crust in her mouth. Though she knew Mary's secret ingredient, the bit of dark chocolate in the filling always surprised her with pleasure.

"Think about it," Mackey continued. "Which would you trust more, a government stamp of approval or a private one?"

"Well, they're both subject to bribery and corruption."

"Yes, but what would happen to *Consumer Reports* if it was revealed that they were taking bribes that influenced their ratings?"

"They'd go out of business."

"And what would happen to a government agency if it was revealed that they were taking bribes that influenced their ratings?"

"Nothing."

"That's right, that's the problem. And it's not the only problem. Government regulations give people a false sense of security. Look what happened with the collapse of the housing market in 2008. People assumed that they could afford the mortgages they were offered, and brokers assumed that the bundled mortgages they were buying were safe and secure because there was plenty of government regulation."

Lorna lingered over the second bite of pie. It was never as good as the first. The surprise was gone. Still, she savored the taste as she introduced whip cream into the mix on her fork. Mary Mackey made her own whip cream, and she added no sugar. So the clean fresh taste of the cream contrasted with the heavy sweetness of the pie.

Pointing with her bare fork, Lorna replied, "Yeah, but Mackey, doesn't this prove the point that we need more government regulation to stop the bad actors who gamed the system, the dishonest mortgage brokers and investment bankers?"

Mackey had heard this before. He didn't miss a beat in responding, "More regulation may have stopped some of the fraud, but it would also have had the unintended consequence of hurting the little guy."

Lorna sipped her coffee and widened her eyes as if to say, *Do tell.*

Mackey continued, "There's been a weird shift in the political debate about regulation. Democrats and liberals used to be against regulation because they saw how only big established companies could afford to comply with regulations—many companies never got started and many other small companies were driven out of business by compliance costs. Now things have changed. Democrats and liberals are calling for more and more regulation, thinking that the rich and powerful need to be reined in before they cause harm."

Lorna put down her coffee. "Don't they have a point,

Mackey?"

"Maybe, but again, the regulation doesn't have to come from government. It's more effective when it comes from an independent private agency. But those kinds of agencies have a hard time getting started when they have to compete with government, which has the force of law. Companies absolutely have to comply with government regulations, so that's where their priority is. But if you take away the government regulations then you have a place for private agencies to evaluate and disseminate information."

Lorna paused, looking for the exquisite experience of the first taste of pie as if she were looking for a word she knew but couldn't quite remember. Coffee, a sip of water, and a bit of cream had nearly cleansed her palate, but the experience of the first taste remained elusive. Putting down her fork, she said, "It still doesn't seem like the government regulation does much harm, though."

Like a bulldog, Mackey was on her, "Come on, Lorna. It does in two senses. One, as I've been saying, it keeps private agencies marginal, and two, it gives people a false sense of security."

"So again, Mackey, doesn't that mean we need more regulation to stop this kind of thing from happening?"

"Not really. What we need is to listen to reason and the voices of reason. While everything was going on, there were plenty of people who were warning that a crash was imminent. The balloon payments would come due for the individual mortgage holders; they wouldn't be able to pay them; and the result would send shockwaves through the system. But no one listened."

"Why not?"

"Because the loudmouths had been right for so long. Unreasonable risks had been paying off and seeming reasonable, and so these mortgages seemed like just another good risk. The people who were warning about the coming disaster were seen as party-poopers, nerds. And they were quiet. They didn't shout.

It wasn't in their nature to shout. They're the kind of people who are coming to North Dakota. They're like you and me, part of the quiet revolution."

Only crust remained on her plate. Far from waste, it was precious for prolonging the experience. Forking some, she replied, "I've heard you say that before, Mackey. But don't you need some loudmouths, some charismatic types who will get people excited and involved?"

"Charisma is good, but we don't want people who are all show and no substance. We want people who speak out because they believe, not because they like the spotlight. That's why we need you, Lorna. You don't want the spotlight, but if you feel compelled to speak, people will listen. Imagine if you had been working for an investment bank and came to realize how risky the whole mortgage situation was. Would you have spoken out?"

Pushing a piece of crust against the roof of her mouth and sweeping it down her throat, she nodded.

"And would people have listened?"

"People do seem to listen to me."

# 15

Chuck Larson continued his tirade against FND through his blog and on talk radio, pointing to the nearly empty Andyne office as a sign that a sinister plot was afoot. Taking action, Mayor Klosterman got the city council to pass a law banning the use of goldens as a means of exchange in the city of Fargo and prohibiting businesses from posting the price of goods and services in goldens. Mackey's Diner, located in Akston, was unaffected, but small businesses in Fargo were targeted. At first, most refused to take down the lists of prices in goldens. Dana Mogck from WDAY News interviewed Todd McFarland, who had come from Minnesota to open his comic-book store.

"This is Dana Mogck reporting live from the Dragon's Den comic-book store in Fargo. I'm with the proprietor Todd McFarland, who has refused to obey the city ordinance banning goldens as a means of exchange. Mr. McFarland, would you please tell the viewers why you refuse to obey the city ordinance?"

"It's simple. There can't be a city ordinance where there is already a federal law," Todd said.

"Please explain."

"It's like the case of Hazleton, Pennsylvania, where the mayor made it illegal to rent an apartment to an illegal alien. The courts ruled that the city had no right to enforce a federal law in such a way."

"So you're saying it's a federal issue?"

"That's right."

"So will you continue to accept goldens as a means of exchange here at the Dragon's Den?"

"Absolutely, and the prices will be listed in goldens until the feds remove them by hand."

Agent Webster Daniels had been urging the people in D.C. to take some action in North Dakota for a long time, but his pleas had fallen on deaf ears. Although Daniels had supported and encouraged Mayor Klosterman, he was surprised when the feds stepped in. In accord with federal law, goldens were declared illegal as a means of exchange, and posting prices in goldens was thereby banned. Glen Summers was ordered to cease and desist in the production and trade of goldens. He was to convert all goldens to dollars immediately.

Lester had never seen Summers shaken before. He stirred his coffee, spilling some on Lester's desk in the Fargo office. Somehow he hadn't anticipated it. Everyone expected the feds to get involved at some point, but goldens seemed safe. In retrospect, Summers blamed himself for not anticipating the interference, telling Lester, "That was exactly the kind of move that we should have expected from the feds."

"But why haven't they come after us for something more serious? Why goldens?" Lester replied.

Summers got up from the chair. "Because people have to be allowed free speech and assembly. They don't want to mess with that, at least not yet. But it's an easy public-relations win to protect the dollar."

"What do you mean?"

"Think about it. What's written on the dollar?"

Leaning back in his chair with his hands behind his head, Lester replied, "In God We Trust."

"That's right. The dollar is surpassed only by the flag as a sacred American symbol. Most people see using another currency as like using another language. It's not fully American. Maybe it's even disloyal. Maybe it's even treasonous."

Lester nodded, and Summers wiped up the coffee he had spilled.

* * *

"Aww, do you feel stressed, Glen?"

"Yes, mistress."

"I know what you need, you need a little release."

"Yes, mistress."

Casey flicked her raven hair and jabbed him with her stiletto boot.

"Well, you won't get it here."

"Yes, mistress."

"I'm going to tease and frustrate you until you're about to burst and then you're going to get dressed and go home."

"Yes, mistress."

# 16

More than three years had passed since Don first came to North Dakota. With his help, FND had gathered the signatures necessary to get the referendum for secession on the November ballot eleven months from now. According to the state constitution, they needed the signatures of 4% of the population for a referendum calling for an amendment to the constitution, and they had greatly exceeded that with over 100,000 signatures.

Reflecting on the frequent-flyer miles she had accumulated over the past three years, Lorna drove to the diner around noon. Later in the day she would have to run some errands and ask her New York doctor to call in a prescription for her birth-control pills. As she pulled into the empty parking lot, Lorna knew something was wrong. The missing glass in the side window didn't register at first, but as she rounded the corner to the front door she saw the graffiti spray painted "GO HOME NORTH DAKOTA IS AMERICA".

Rushing in, she called, "Don, Don."

Mackey emerged from the side, saying, "He's in the back, darlin'."

"Is he all right?"

"Yeah, everyone's all right."

"Was it a bomb?"

"No, just rocks."

"Who did it?"

Mackey shrugged. Don pushed through the kitchen door, and Lorna leaped to embrace him, saying, "Oh my God. I'm so glad you're OK."

"Just fine. Nothing happened while we were here. Must have been in the middle of the night, right, Mack?"

Mackey nodded and pursed his lips, as the wind whistled through the broken widows.

"What can I do to help?" Lorna asked.

"Wear the apron," Mackey said.

"No, I mean to clean up the place and get things running."

"I'll take care of that," Mackey said, "but we need you for other things."

Don blanched, saying, "The apron is mine."

Mackey looked the other way and said, "You've learned what you needed to, and your blogging is where you serve best."

Don untied the apron and threw it at the back of Mackey's head before pushing through the door into the kitchen.

"I'm a liability," Lorna said, "and besides, I'm not fully convinced."

"Wear the apron, pour the coffee, listen, learn, lead. Don did his tour, and now we need you."

"Need me how?" she asked, shifting her weight to her right foot.

"You're an asset."

"I'm an asset? How?"

"You'll see."

Mackey picked up the apron and handed it to Lorna.

"You don't have to put it on now," Mackey said. "Go home and get some rest. I'll see you first thing tomorrow."

Lorna had distanced herself from business, leaving day-to-day operations in the hands of her second-in-command. Kamala had come up in the world much as Lorna had, beginning as a call girl and moving into administration. Lorna had delegated a lot of responsibility to Kamala over the years, putting her in charge of special interests and fantasy encounters. Lorna didn't have patience for guys who wanted costumes worn and dramas acted out, so she let Kamala develop that end of the business. It had been a raging success, bringing in a whole new set of customers. Kamala kept a healthy commission for that business and had saved her money in anticipation of starting her own escort service. Of course Lorna expected that she would not just want to leave one day, but would want to take girls and customers with her. Kamala could have done that easily during any of Lorna's extended stays in North Dakota, but she hadn't, at least not yet. So, with the apron on, Lorna sold the business to Kamala, the name, the website, the apartments, all of it. Kamala was surprised, but not shocked.

"What are you going to do, Lorna, open a shop there?" she asked.

Lorna paused to adjust the phone and look out the window before replying, "Maybe, but not now. I want to be a part of what's happening here."

"Be careful, Lorna. It's not some kind of cult, is it?"

"No, it's not a cult, it's not even a group. It's just a bunch of people joined together by wanting to be left alone."

"I don't get it, Lorna. But if it makes you happy, that's what matters."

"Thanks," she said looking down at the floor.

"You deserve a break or a mid-life crisis or whatever this is."

"Yeah, I don't know what it is, but I want to be with Don and I want to be here. I want to make something grow."

Before the vandalism Lorna had become a regular at Mackey's Diner, sitting at the counter and talking for hours each day with the FND folks who came in for sustenance and reassurance. Don and Mackey knew she had a gift, and Don had always believed that gift could be transplanted into practically any business or operation. Lorna was even more magnetic than Mackey. Well before she put on the apron and started pouring coffee, people were coming to talk to Lorna.

The diner had always been the Mecca for FND members, but with Lorna holding court, a new crowd began to come as well, natives who were curious about FND. They were impressed with Mackey's turn-the-other-cheek response to the vandalism, and word spread of the blonde oracle who poured coffee. A farmer named Klaus Schmidt suggested to Lorna that the even though the vandalism was bad for Mackey it was good for the economy because it stimulated things, put money in motion.

"By that reasoning, we should break some more windows and smash some furniture while we're at it," Lorna said as she filled Schmidt's coffee.

Schmidt adjusted his back and then leaned forward, placing his elbows on the counter, resting the knuckles of his right hand in the palm of his left. Her voice threw him. It was small, high pitched, and nasal. Almost a child's voice. "Well, no," he said. "I just mean that there's a silver lining in this case. It was awful to deal with the destruction, but it was good for the glass maker and the installer and the repair guys and everyone else who got work out of the situation."

Over the chattering crowd, Roger Daltrey sang on the radio "won't get fooled again."

"Think a little further," Lorna said. Schmidt made a face like he had smelled something bad. So Lorna continued, "Yes, it's good for them, but it's bad for everyone else who won't get work now that Mackey's money got diverted to cleaning up the damage."

"What do you mean?" Schmidt asked, taking his elbows off the counter. He had a hard time making sense of his own reaction. Lorna's voice made him want to take care of her, but she didn't need to be taken care of.

Lorna bent down to look Schmidt in the eye. "Well, Mackey had a deductible on the insurance. So the first three thousand dollars of damages he had to pay out of his own pocket. It's not as if he just had three thousand dollars lying around. He had to divert money that he was going to use for improvements in the kitchen, for a new fryer and some other things. So the people he was going to buy the fryer from lost out."

Schmidt stole a peek at Lorna's cleavage while she was

speaking, and he could only manage to respond by saying, "OK but still, most of the damage was covered by insurance."

"Yeah, but that means the insurance company lost out. Instead of taking that money as profit and spending it on something they genuinely wanted they were compelled to use it to clean up an unnecessary mess in Mackey's Diner. So in the end money has been diverted to clean up a mess rather than being spent on something that people genuinely want, something that has earned their business."

Schmidt put his thumbs under his suspenders and squinted. It wasn't just the sound of her voice. It was her delivery, with its rising and falling intonations, and it was the unexpected intelligence.

"All right, miss, that may be true of this situation. But what about on the larger scale when big companies are forced to make repairs and put their money in motion?"

"Same thing. No one is keeping their money out of circulation under a mattress. Large companies and wealthy individuals have their money invested or in savings. This puts the money at the disposal of other companies in whom they invest or at the disposal of banks who keep only a fraction in reserve and put the rest of the money into circulation via loans."

Schmidt started to speak but then silenced himself by sipping on his coffee.

Lorna resumed, saying, "You can't stimulate the economy by breaking windows. It may look that way because you see a flurry of activity in response, but you need to keep in mind what you don't see, the people who are deprived of business as a result, people like you, who lose grain sales."

"What do you know about grain sales?"

"Nothing, but I'd like to learn. What's the most important thing about running a farm that people like me don't know?"

Lorna leaned in, putting her elbows on the counter and bumping her fists together. Schmidt moved his eyes from her cleavage to her eyes and began to tell her about how growing and harvesting the crop was only the beginning of what he did.

Klaus Schmidt didn't go away convinced that day, but he did come back.

\* \* \*

"You must think you're quite the bad ass."

"No, mistress."

"Don't contradict me."

"Yes, mistress."

She strutted across the room.

"You know how Mistress Casey likes to be paid, right?"

"Yes, mistress."

"How, Agent Daniels?"

"In goldens, mistress."

"But thanks to you and your friends, that's not possible anymore, is it?"

"No, mistress."

"So you're going to have to find a new way to pay me, aren't you?"

"Yes, mistress."

"Do you know the only thing more valuable than gold, Agent Daniels?"

"No, mistress."

"It's information. You're going to start giving me information."

\* \* \*

Heads turned when he walked in to the sound of "Sweet Home Alabama" on the radio. You didn't see too many black guys in Mackey's Diner. Hell, you didn't see many black guys anywhere in North Dakota. With his glasses and Brooks Brothers suit, he didn't look like a troublemaker, though, certainly not of the African-American variety. Lester took a seat in a booth and ordered ham and eggs from Mary Mackey. The first cup of coffee went down quickly.

"Refill?" Lorna asked.

"Yes, please."

"You must be Lester."

"How would you ever know that?"

"I wonder?" Her eyes had him. "Mackey tells me you head things up at Andyne in Fargo. How's that going?"

"Pretty well. Our numbers were down last quarter, but I think we're headed in the right direction again."

"I used to know some guys at Andyne in New York."

"How?"

"Work."

"Were you in banking?"

"No, I was a whore, and then a madam."

Lester flinched. "I see."

"Yeah, so confidentiality precludes any mention of who."

Lester smiled. "Of course. There must be a strict professional code of ethics."

Lorna turned to continue her refill rounds.

"Wait a second, Lorna. Don't I know you?"

"It's quite possible," she said with a smile, "but I think I'd remember."

"No, I mean did you go to NYU?"

"I did indeed."

"I knew I recognized you. You worked in the bookstore on Bleecker Street, right?"

"That was me."

"Small world."

"It's about to get smaller."

"How do you mean?

Without asking, Lorna took a seat in the booth across from

Lester and put the coffee pot on the table. "Secession is going to shrink things. Think about it. Half a million people who want to be free, who want to be left alone, have come together to make that happen. There are bound to be connections that people didn't expect."

"Why did Mackey want me to meet you? I mean I'm glad. But I know he's not playing cupid."

"No, that's right. I'm involved with someone—Don Jenkins, the writer."

"So what did Mackey have in mind?"

"I don't know, Lester. Maybe you're in my karass?"

"Karass?" Lester wrinkled his forehead. "Vonnegut?"

"That's right, Lester. *Cat's Cradle.* You know it?"

"It's one of my favorite books. I thought about majoring in English in college. But what kind of job could you get with that degree?"

"You could have become a whore."

Lester raised his eyebrows and took off his glasses. "You majored in English?"

"Yeah, but it was law school that turned me into a whore. I realized it was nobler than being a lawyer. And I liked it, and I was good at it."

Lester crooked his neck back and looked at the ceiling for a moment.

"And so, what, then you went into business for yourself, became a madam?"

"That's right. I ran a high end—pardon the pun—escort service. In fact I was running it from North Dakota until a few weeks ago."

Lester laughed.

Mary Mackey brought the ham and eggs. Lester cut the ham and before taking a bite asked, "Now you're a waitress? Step down, isn't it?"

"No, I'm a coffee whore. I just refill coffee."

"Why?"

"Because no one has just one cup of coffee. They need refills."

"Ha! No, I mean why are you doing this job? And why do you call yourself that?"

"Do you ever refer to yourself as a nigger?"

Lester's nostrils flared and he closed his eyes. "Yes, sometimes."

"Why do you do that?"

Lester put down his fork. "To take the sting away, to take back the word."

"Same reason here. I could call myself a courtesan, or an escort, or a call girl, or whatever. But why should I do that? I'm not embarrassed by what I've done for a living. You can call me a whore if you want to. Can I call you a nigger?"

Lester winced. "Certainly not."

"I didn't think so."

"And do you have any desire to call me a whore after I've already called myself a whore?"

"No."

"Well then, it works." Lorna got up to leave.

"Wait. But why are you here serving coffee?"

"I don't know. I was hoping you could tell me that, I mean, if you're part of my karass and all." She winked.

"So let me remember, Lorna. The karass is a group that we're a part of that serves some higher purpose."

"Yes, that's right, according to Bokoninism."

"And Bokoninism is a made-up religion that says all religions are bullshit, including Bokoninism."

"That's right."

"And you're an adherent of Bokoninism."

Lorna sat down again, saying, "I'm a devout Bokoninist."

"Which means that you believe Bokoninism is utter and complete bullshit?"

"Of course, Lester. Bokoninism exists only in a book, and even in the book it's acknowledged to be bullshit."

"So why do you think I'm part of your karass?"

Lorna leaned in, exposing her cleavage. "Because we have to believe in something, even if we know it's complete bullshit. It's like going to the movies to see a science-fiction film. There's nothing more annoying than when the person you're with repeatedly sticks you with their elbow and says, 'That couldn't happen.' Of course it couldn't happen. It's make believe, so play along. That's the point."

Lester put his elbows on the table. "So we need to believe we're in each other's karass?"

"The fate of the world depends on it."

"Ha!"

"No, I'm serious, Lester. Look at all these people coming to North Dakota. What do they all have in common?"

"Well, I'd guess they want government off their backs. They want to be free."

"Yeah, yeah. But I mean what do they have in common as people?"

"I don't know, Lorna, what?"

"They're loners. Well not exactly loners, but individualists. They're porcupines; the quills sticking out of their backs tell you to leave them alone."

Lester put his glasses back on. "That's true. That's the atmosphere at Andyne. The people who moved to North Dakota before we set up the office liked doing their own thing on their own time. So when I set up the office in Fargo I let them all telecommute from wherever they were in North Dakota. No one is required to actually come into the office. It's a R.O.W.E.—a results-only work environment. As long as they get their work done, that's all that matters."

Lorna's eyes widened. "How's that working out?"

"I don't know. Numbers were up for a while. Employees really seem to run well on intrinsic motivation. They appreciate being treated as players, not pawns. But now something seems to be missing. Our numbers were down last quarter."

"You need to preach the gospel of Bokoninism."

"Seriously?"

Lorna smirked. "No, not seriously, not literally. I'm not saying that you should make all your employees read *Cat's Cradle*."

"What are you saying?"

"You're part of my karass. You should be able to figure it out."

Lester took off his glasses and widened his eyes. "People need to feel like they belong to something, even if it's bullshit, is that it?"

Lorna smiled. "That's it. Look around this diner. Why do people come here?"

"I don't know. I never come here. The ham and eggs are pretty good, but I bet that they come to talk to you."

"I've only been a coffee whore for a few months. This place is an institution."

"Well, then they come to hear Mackey."

"Yup, that has a lot to do with it. That's why people started coming here. They could tell Mackey anything and he would listen. He wouldn't say much, but they would walk away knowing what they had to do."

"So is Mackey part of our karass?"

"I don't know. You don't get to find out for sure who was part of your karass until you die and go to Heaven, Lester."

"But there is no Heaven, right?"

"Right."

"So people come here for Mackey?"

"No, of course not. They come here because this is a church. Mackey may be the high priest, but people don't just want a shepherd. They want other sheep."

"Are you calling these people sheep?"

Lorna grimaced. "Certainly not. They're cats. You can't herd cats. Cats just want to be left alone, but occasionally they enjoy the company of other cats. They need to play with each other and feel a part of something so that they can then enjoy being left alone again."

"That actually makes sense, Lorna."

"Maybe."

"What do you mean, maybe?"

"Well, it's just a bunch of bullshit that I made up as we were talking. I mean first I told you they were porcupines, then sheep, and then cats. You can't just accept everything I say."

She had him. He was sure that he was part of her karass. Lester drove back to Fargo in a fog. He could have sat at the diner all day in conversation with Lorna, but she just walked away after telling him that it was all bullshit. That was the key. Bullshit is bad. But if you acknowledge bullshit as bullshit, then it becomes good, useful, essential.

Lester remembered vaguely that in *Cat's Cradle* the dictator who ran the island of San Lorenzo had an ongoing agreement with Bokonin: Bokonin would be the enemy of the state and it would be the first priority of the state to capture and kill Bokonin, who was living in the jungle, always just beyond the grasp of the state. Of course the agreement was that Bokonin would never really be captured. The dictator was himself a devout Bokoninist. They needed each other as fictional enemies. All of the people of San Lorenzo were devout Bokoninists, despite the fact, or because of the fact, that Bokoninism was outlawed.

The lesson for FND was what? That it needed an enemy? It already had an enemy: the U.S. government. But the government hadn't been acting like much of an enemy. Aside from shutting down the trade in goldens, the government hadn't done much to stop the secession. What did that mean? Were they not taking FND seriously? Were they willing to let North Dakota go? Were they working behind the scenes? None of it was clear, and none of it was what Mackey and the FND leadership had expected. It was like the cat's cradle, the string game from which the book took its name. When you look at the string figure you don't see a cat and you don't see a cradle. So why do they call it a cat's cradle? Who knows?

\* \* \*

Don had spent the day not writing. No matter how he pushed and strained, not even a blog would come out. That night in bed Lorna told Don about the day's conversations, saying, "I like pouring coffee. It gives me a reason to be there, not just hanging out at the counter."

Don scowled. "Wearing the apron makes you a target. Lots of kooks like Ronnie Black come in, just wanting to sip coffee and explain their pet theory about how the black helicopters are watching them and the UN is conspiring to put a world government in place."

Lorna rolled over and sighed. "Yeah, today one of the North Dakota State kids gave me the whole run down on how hemp can save the environment, how the government and the car companies are in cahoots with the oil companies to keep hemp fuel off the market."

"If you need a day off, just say the word."

"Nah, I'm OK, but why don't you at least come by the diner?"

"Yeah, I'll do that some time, but not tomorrow. Has anyone been asking for me?"

Lorna lied. "All the time."

"You know, I was really good at that job."

"You were the best, but..."

"But what?"

"Things are changing."

"What the fuck does that mean?"

## 17

Everyone at Andyne thought Lester Naylor was tall, but he was only five-foot-ten. It must have been his posture. Lester was a golden boy, but with due caution, no one used those words to describe him. Having risen through the corporate ranks in record time, Lester was now devoted to establishing Andyne in North Dakota. He had spearheaded the program that allowed Andyne employees to relocate and telecommute from North Dakota, and he relocated himself with the opening of the first Andyne office in Fargo. The potential advantages of making North Dakota Andyne's new corporate home were obvious. If North Dakota seceded, Andyne would escape corporate income tax and no longer have to pay an army of tax accountants and tax lawyers.

Lester had grown up in Brooklyn and won admission to New York City's most prestigious public high school, Stuyvesant. There he found himself a distinct minority among a population dominated by Asians and Jews. His friend Rashid complained, "It's not fair," pointing at the two of them and then waving at the sea of Asians in the cafeteria.

"What's not fair?" Lester asked.

"Are you blind? We're only 1% of this place."

"What's unfair about that?" Lester replied.

"The population of New York is 19% African-American."

"So?"

"So that means the student body should be 19% African-American."

"But everyone took the same entrance exam."

"Doesn't matter, fool. Most black kids go to stank-ass junior highs."

"Yeah, but what about all these Asian kids? No one's givin' them a break, and the school is over 70% Asian."

"Their parents are always on their ass, and they work like

crazy. Half of them are in the library now, not even eatin' lunch."

"Maybe that's what we should do."

In fact, that's what Lester started doing, eating quickly and spending the rest of the lunch period in the library. That didn't bring up his class rank much, but it might have kept it from falling. When it came time to apply to college, Lester's guidance counselor, Mrs. Siegel, told him to "be shoo-er to take advantage of affirmative action."

"What do you mean?" Lester asked.

"Check the bawx that indicates you're African-American. That's as good as another 200 points on the SAT."

"Why do I get 200 points for checking a box?"

"Because."

"Because why?"

"You're disadvantaged."

"No I'm not."

"Oh, Lester, shoo-er you are. It's not easy to be African-American."

"How would you know?"

"Well, my tribe hasn't exactly had it easy in this country either."

"Did anyone give you an extra 200 SAT points?"

"Well no, but..."

"Then I don't want them either."

Lester thought about leaving the box unchecked, but instead he checked "Caucasian" on his applications. Lester had a sure chance of admission to Harvard if he had checked the box properly, but instead Lester went to NYU and majored in business administration. He had begun with the intent of majoring in economics, but he found that what passed for economics was myopic. So after the basic courses in macro and micro, he moved into the generalized business major. Again though, he was disappointed in what he learned, much preferring his required courses in history and literature.

In the living room of a meticulous apartment in the Samuel J. Tilden housing project, Lester's mother asked him, "What's litracher?"

"English, Mom."

She laughed, saying, "You can't get no job with no Anglish and no hiss-tree."

"But lots of kids major in those subjects, Mom."

"Those is rich kids, whose daddies get 'em fancy jobs. You got a big rich daddy I don't know about?"

"No, ma'am, you're right."


Colleagues often misread Lester's quiet for cunning, and they were careful what they said around him in a way that they weren't with other people. So Lester was surprised when Glen Summers started visiting his office to tell him about what was going on in North Dakota. People who were fed up with the alternatives were declaring their personal independence and moving with the plan of declaring state independence. Summers realized it was the kind of bold yet obvious solution to a problem that Lester had become known for at Andyne. When other people said "you can't do that" Lester reacted with "why not?" They would have no reason, just "it's not done." So Lester would do it anyway, and often it would work. In some cases, like with the Pensky portfolio, his bold moves worked because people just let them play out. Lester realized he got this latitude because he was black, but he didn't feel badly about it. He wasn't succeeding because of preferential treatment; he was succeeding because of other people's lack of vision or excess of diffidence.

It was Lester who came up with the idea of encouraging Andyne employees to move to North Dakota. The company had an interest in establishing an office there, and the best way to do that was to get employees to move on their own. Once there were enough employees, if conditions were still auspicious, Andyne could open an office. Of course, lots of employees would rather move to other states where Andyne did not have offices, like Virginia, Oregon, and Arizona, but there was no company interest in supporting such moves. On a case-by-case basis, some individual moves with telecommuting agreements were made, but North Dakota had the only blanket policy. Any employee who wanted to move there could keep their job by telecommuting, in anticipation of the time when a corporate office would open.

The policy had been in place for a year when Lester Naylor himself moved to North Dakota. Over a thousand Andyne employees had moved, and Glen Summers was splitting his time between Fargo and New York. The Andyne immigrants were routinely accused of being racists. "Those crazies moving to North Dakota are just looking to get away from blacks and other minorities." So Lester was cast in the role of race traitor. He was accustomed to this from growing up in the Brownsville section of Brooklyn and commuting to Stuyvesant High School in Manhattan. Malik, Tyree, and other neighborhood kids called him an Oreo and accused him of "acting white" because he read books and spoke grammatically correct English. The Oreo label and "acting white" struck Lester as funny because many white kids, as far as he could tell, were busy "acting black." So the whitest way to act would be to act black. If anything, he was "acting Asian." Lester understood the herd mentality that chastened him for doing his own thing. At its core was fear and self-preservation, understandable in itself but not the kind of thing that would deter him.

It hurt, though, when Shaunika, La-sondra, and the other girls in the neighborhood gave him grief for dating Liza Cohen. There had been some grudging admiration among the girls, and certainly among their mothers, for Lester's journey from the hood to Stuyvesant. "That boy's gonna make somethin' of hisself," they would say. When he brought a white girl home with him to study, though, all sympathy was lost. Lester was just another brother who thought he was too good for a black woman. Malik and Tyree were envious and anxious to meet Liza, but afterwards they just laughed, saying, "That Jew is butt-ugly." At around the same time, Lester started wearing glasses. He had probably needed them for years, but in studying German, his poor eyesight became apparent. Lester's mind could not fill in the fuzzy places with a foreign language the way it could with English. The glasses looked like an affectation to the kids in the hood, though. What sixteen-year-old kid needed reading glasses? None of it registered with Lester, or it barely registered, much as it barely registered with Liza why some of her family and friends found it offensive that she was studying German.

So Lester was accustomed to other blacks labeling him, but North Dakota brought the new experience of being labeled a hypocrite and an Uncle Tom by whites. Others had probably thought it before at NYU and in liberal white circles, but no one had ever expressed it directly. Now Lester was being labeled a token and a stooge by the forces opposing FND. Lester received hate mail, most of it anonymous, asking what his price was and how could he sleep at night. At first it surprised him. He couldn't believe that people would question his motives in that way. Why was it so important to see him as black? And then to see him as for sale?

Summers was the closest thing to a mentor that he had, and Summers certainly had not prepared him for this. Lester saw himself as like Summers, smart and hard working. Lester was smart, very smart, but that was not his favorite quality about himself. He had known a lot of very smart kids at Stuyvesant and at NYU, but he felt sorry for many of them because they would never amount to much. Lester's favorite quality was his discipline. His mother was his inspiration. She never missed a day's work, and she kept the apartment sparkling in the midst of squalor. The problem with his mother, though, was that she had gotten discipline late in life after having children without getting married and without finding a career. His mother didn't preach discipline; she just talked about "doin' wha's right."

At Stuyvesant, Lester saw discipline as well as the complete lack of it. Many of the Vietnamese, Korean, and Chinese kids had it. They would get to school early and study in the library; they would never go out to lunch, instead bringing noodles from home to be eaten quickly before going to the library for the lunch hour. Many helped the family business after school, working the register at the convenience store or take-out place, and then staying up late studying. These were the athletes of the mind, the ones who never let their mental muscles get flabby. Lester fed off their energy. He was never discouraged if he didn't do as well as they did. He just worked harder and longer. On the other side, he saw plenty of kids who were at least as smart as any of the Asians and yet who couldn't get themselves to work. They would cram, cheat, take short cuts. In subjects where they were particularly gifted they could cruise a bit, but by senior year a gulf had opened between them and the hard workers. Hard work and discipline outperform intelligence and natural ability over the long run. This was one lesson he could not have learned at the local high school in Brooklyn where smart kids skated by unchallenged.

Lester was in his early thirties and without any sense of political identity when Summers started talking to him. They were an unlikely pair, Glen Summers, a short white patrician from Westchester and Lester Naylor, a tall black guy from Brooklyn. But after watching Lester for six months, Summers sensed they were the same.

In Lester's little office, Summers said, "Guys like us aren't interested in politics, and we have to get over the feeling that there's something wrong with us because of it."

Lester took off his glasses, scratched his right eyebrow, and tilted his head left.

Summers continued, "Makes sense, right? People seem morally superior because they're concerned with how the government can make things better. Guys like us feel guilty for not caring."

"Shouldn't we care?" Lester leaned forward, putting his elbows on his desk.

Summers gestured at the seat in front of Lester's desk. "May I?"

"Of course."

Summers sat and continued, "No. Guys like us know that government and politicians should do as little as possible. We want to be left alone. We don't want the government to tell us what we can eat, drink, smoke, or fuck. And we definitely don't want the government to take part of our property and give it to someone else in the name of social justice. Helping others is the role of private charity."

Lester nodded and said, "That's right. But I've always felt like a bad person for thinking those things."

"You're not a bad person, Lester. You're a libertarian."

Lester's eyes brightened. "OK. Tell me more."

"Democrats have convinced people that we need protection from free-market capitalism and Republicans have convinced people that government needs to legislate morality."

"So what can be done?" Lester asked.

"Nothing. Nothing in this country," Summers replied.

# 18

Ken Merkel always wore a cowboy hat, but he had never been to Texas. In fact, he had never been outside the Dakotas. Standing six-foot-five in his boots, he was an imposing figure as he walked in the door of Mackey's Diner to meet the woman he heard was ruling the roost. The smell of bacon and sausage filled the air as Merkel took a seat at the counter. Mackey was in the back helping the cooks with the breakfast rush, and Renata took Merkel's order for a meat lover's omelet with cheese. The first cup went down quickly, and he was getting antsy when Lorna appeared to refill him.

"Thanks, little lady," he said.

Lorna smiled brightly and nodded.

Just before she turned to walk away, Merkel asked, "What's this I hear about succession?"

Lorna winked at him. "Secession. The idea is that North Dakota will leave the United States and be its own independent nation."

Merkel thought he detected a Southern accent. "But that's impossible. That was all settled with the Civil War. States cannot succeed from the Union."

On the radio Steven Tyler sang about kings and queens and guillotines.

"You're correct," Lorna said.

Merkel's satisfied smile disappeared when she continued, "Segregation was the law for nearly 100 years after the Civil War, but that didn't make it right."

Merkel glowered. "This is different. States can't succeed. That's to protect the sanctity of the Union."

Lorna put down the coffeepot. "I'm not sure who it protects. It just takes away a choice, an option."

"Listen, miss, certain options have to be off the table."

"But why?"

"Because certain things ain't right."

"OK, sir, but how is a state's right to choose its membership in a nation something that ain't right?"

"Because there has to be an authority and there has to be respect for authority."

Renata placed the meat lover's omelet in front of Merkel. He cut in without acknowledging the waitress and without taking his eyes off Lorna. Her poreless skin and dewy complexion seemed somehow unreal. Yet the harder he looked the more natural it appeared. Aside from eyeliner, she wasn't wearing makeup.

Lorna put her hand on her chin. "So the government is in charge?"

"Right, the government's in charge."

Without looking down at his food and without switching the fork to his right hand, Merkel put a piece of the omelet in his mouth. The ham cradled the sausage and a thin layer of cheese separated the bacon. All was separate and yet all formed a whole.

"So does the government serve the people?" Lorna asked. "Or do the people serve the government?"

"Both. It works both ways," he said as he swallowed.

Lorna put her elbows on the counter and leaned in. "All right, but where does the government get its authority? Doesn't the government derive its authority from the consent of the people?"

Merkel willed his eyes away from her cleavage. "Yes, but it's like a marriage. It's forever."

Lorna stood up and stepped back, saying, "But half of all marriages end in divorce."

"Yeah, and that's not such a good thing, is it, miss?"

"Call me Lorna."

"All right, Lorna, you can call me Ken." As he pressed the bacon and cheese against the roof of his mouth he hated to swallow it, to lose that moment, that unique taste. If he didn't, though, it would become sweet and nauseating with saliva. After coffee washed away what remained, Ken continued, "Now divorce ain't such a good thing, is it?"

Lorna warmed his cup and asked, "So should divorce be against the law, Ken?"

"No, but it oughta be a lot less common."

"Oh, I agree," she said. "Will you tell me what you think of this?" Before Merkel could reply, she asked, "Would having arranged marriages make divorce less common? I mean parents could coordinate ideal matches for their children."

Scrunching his face like he was in pain, Merkel replied, "No, and that's got nothin' to do with it."

Lorna paused to look upward as if the words and thoughts were descending on her. Then, looking Merkel straight in the eye, she said, "But isn't that like the situation we have in this country? You're born a citizen and you're stuck with it unless you want to leave and live in another country."

Merkel stretched back on his stool and then exhaled, letting his gut tumble over his belt buckle. "No, miss, that's not exactly so. Besides, you can change the laws of this country if you don't like 'em."

The chatter around them in the diner concerned the charges of bribery and corruption against the Speaker of the House. Everyone knew that Washington was dominated by lobbyists representing special interests, and everyone realized that money talked. Yet everyone on cable news pretended to be shocked when it came out that Prallman had funneled millions into the Speaker's accounts in the Cayman Islands. The Speaker was still in the denial stage, insisting he had done nothing wrong.

With sincere skepticism Lorna asked, "But what if you try to change the laws and can't get it done?"

Without missing a beat, Merkel replied, "Then love it or leave it."

"OK," Lorna said.

"OK?"

"Yeah, OK," she said. "That's what we're trying to do. We're trying to leave. But we don't want to go to Canada, or Mexico, or France. We want a piece of land to start our own country."

"But you can't do that," he said. "You can't just take part of this country and go."

Lorna breathed deeply and then, smiling, asked, "Why not, Ken? Because the government says so?"

"That's right."

"Even if we have a majority of the vote? A state still can't decide to leave?"

"No. That's treason."

"But doesn't the government's authority derive from the consent of the governed?

"Yes, that's right."

"The government works for us, doesn't it? We don't work for them, right?"

"That's true, miss, but there has to be some respect for authority and tradition."

"Like God, right, Ken?"

"How do you mean?" Merkel cracked his knuckles.

Lorna continued, "God has the authority to tell us that we must obey him, right?"

"Of course," he said.

Lorna leaned over, resting her elbows on the counter and her chin on her laced fingers. "And you say the nation has the authority to tell us we must obey?"

"Yeah, that's right," Merkel said.

"But isn't that making the nation into God?"

"Now that's blasphemy. Don't put words in my mouth. I'm just sayin' that there has to be some authority. Parents have authority over their children. That kinda thing."

Lorna looked him in the eye. "So, are we children? Is the

government like our parents? They get to tell us what we can and cannot do?"

"In a way, yeah."

Lorna pulled back her elbows, stood up straight and folded her arms. "I'm nobody's mother. But children don't stay children forever. Whether it's at 18 or 21 they get to make decisions for themselves. So when do we outgrow the authority of the government and get to make decisions for ourselves?"

"It don't work like that," he said. "You're mixing things up."

"So it's more like a marriage? 'Til death do us part?"

"Yeah, that's what I was saying before, miss."

"And the government is like the husband and the people are like the wife?"

Merkel ate the last bite of his omelet more quickly than he wanted to, forgetting to savor it. Annoyed, he asked, "How do you mean?"

"The people pledge to love, honor, and obey."

"Don't get all feminist on me now. You know that's not part of the marriage vows anymore."

"But it seems to be part of the citizen's obligation," Lorna said, unfolding her arms and turning he palms upward.

"Well, yeah, up to a point," Merkel said, concealing his mouth behind his coffee cup.

Lorna turned to fill the cups of the two customers sitting to Merkel's right, and then replied, "But where is that point? And how do we know when we've passed it? God can insist on absolute obedience. He's God, after all. But if a government derives its power to govern from the consent of the governed, when a majority of the governed decide to withdraw that consent, what right does the government have to say, 'No, you can't do that?'"

"Listen, miss, you're talkin' treason. There just has to be some laws, some authority, or else everything would be anarchy and chaos."

"I'm not so sure about that, Ken," Lorna said, putting the coffeepot down on the counter. "Or at least I'm not so sure what laws or authority we need to have. But obviously you're a smart guy. You've thought a lot about these things. Let's talk some more some time."

All heads at the counter turned to watch as Lorna walked away.

# 19

Don found no relief for his writer's block. Spending eight hours a day pouring coffee refills had stimulated him, but now that he was in his apartment all day he couldn't get himself to write anything worthwhile. So he played a lot of *Tetris* and surfed the web, waiting for Lorna to come home. When he heard Lorna at the door, Don dashed to his desk and pretended to write.

"Honey, I'm home!" Lorna called.

"Shh. Just a minute, I'm in the middle of a thought. I have to get this sentence down."

After typing some nonsense into his computer, Don frowned and said, "It's not easy."

"What's not easy?"

"Writing," he said, while closing the document.

Lorna walked up behind him and started rubbing his shoulders. "Why don't you come by the diner tomorrow? It's good inspiration."

"Yeah, sure, maybe."

"You miss the apron, don't you?"

Don stared straight ahead at the computer screen and said, "Don't be silly. I have more important things to do. Besides, it's your turn, right?"

Lorna didn't answer. So Don asked, "What does Mackey say?"

"He says I'm good for business."

"I bet you are."

"Jealous?"

"No."

Don stood up and walked to the window.

"A little?"

"Maybe."

"Hmm. Tell Mama."

Don turned to face her. "Everyone gets this smart, sexy, sassy waitress. It's the sass, right? You make them all feel like fascinating bad boys."

"Of course. That's how they want to think of themselves. So I help them do it."

"That's it? What's the next move?"

"I don't know. For now, I'm learning and I'm having fun. And if my old man boyfriend would get off my back, that would be enough."

* * *

Summers was still smarting from the federal crackdown on goldens when they met at the diner.

"You knew it was going to happen," Mackey said.

Summers threw his napkin on top of his plate. "Yeah, but I thought it would happen when other things happened. It was being singled out that shook me."

Mackey scratched his chest and folded his arms. "Get over it, Summers. You don't hear me crying about how they vandalized this place."

"I'm over it."

"Doesn't seem like it."

"I can't help how it seems to you. The important thing is that there's a market for it, and we'll have our own currency after secession. Once the black rain starts falling things will be golden."

# 20

The White House needed to stop the secession without violating anyone's rights to free speech or assembly. If action had been taken earlier, then the situation would have been more manageable. No one, apparently including the FND members themselves, had predicted that FND would attract so many members so quickly.

The deep freeze of February had set in, and a vote on secession was scheduled for November. By all appearances they had the numbers. The only way to stop the secession short of declaring it illegal and unconstitutional was to outnumber FND by moving more people to North Dakota. The federal government couldn't just order citizens to move to North Dakota. And even though many Americans strongly opposed the secession of North Dakota, they wouldn't be willing to uproot their lives and move there to prevent the secession. As Webster Daniels knew, there was only one option now: the military. The federal government would have to station fifty thousand troops in North Dakota in time for the election. According to North Dakota state law, a member of the military who is stationed in North Dakota for at least thirty days is eligible to vote in a state election. So the move would need to be complete by the beginning of October. The Pentagon put plans in motion.

There were a number of military bases in North Dakota, including the Air Force base in Grand Forks and the one in Minot that houses nuclear weapons. But there were not nearly enough facilities to house fifty thousand troops. So it would be a matter of setting up camp. The goal was to have a peaceful, democratic solution. In addition to reassigning troops from bases in the continental U.S., troops could be drawn down from bases in Europe and Japan.

* * *

In her suburban home, Sarah Andersen had not followed the story in great detail, but what she knew she did not like. These people seemed selfish and greedy. They didn't like paying taxes or supporting social programs, and they wanted to legalize drugs, gambling, and prostitution. To get what they wanted they were prepared to break up the United States.

So when the orders came that her Minnesota reserve unit was to deploy to North Dakota, Sarah was glad to be a part of the mission. Officially they would be there to keep the peace, but unofficially they were being sent to vote in the November election and stop the secession. She knew this, as did everyone else in the military. The commanders could not tell them how to vote, but they could certainly count on Sarah's support. Like most members of the military, she was genuinely patriotic. What was being asked of Sarah and her military colleagues was a small sacrifice to preserve the sacred Union.

Dr. Ben Andersen was not pleased to see his wife deployed, but he was comforted by the fact that the tour of duty in North Dakota would be brief. Most of the fifty thousand troops would be living in temporary facilities. No one, including the commanders, wanted to be there long. As soon as the referendum on secession was defeated and things were stable, Sarah would be back home in her civilian job as a nurse at the hospital.

* * *

Mackey spread the word about the military deployment long before it was on the news. "How do you know?" Shelly Robinson asked.

"I have a very good source."

"Those bastards are smart," Shelly said, sitting at the counter eating her second piece of apple pie with cheddar cheese.

Mackey nodded. Shelly Robinson drove a black van with her logo painted in hot pink, "The Pink Plunger Plumbing and Heating Services." Two years ago she had moved The Pink Plunger from Pittsburgh to Fargo even though the business had been a rousing success in Pittsburgh.

After ten years of working for Vance Plumbing and Heating in Pittsburgh, Shelly had saved enough money to go out on her own. What appeared to be her greatest liability was actually her greatest asset. Out of solidarity, women liked hiring her. Men, though, were the key to Shelly's success because men were intimidated by other men. Calling in a plumber to fix the pipes was emasculating, and most plumbers did nothing to lessen the experience. They felt the need to point out the problem and explain the solution in a way that only left the male homeowner feeling worse. During her years working for Vance, Shelly noticed that men felt more at ease with her, especially when she was working alone. She was the oddball in their eyes, a female plumber. They could feel good about themselves and their ineptitude in comparison to this strange woman.

Within two years of operation in Pittsburgh, Shelly had more business than she could handle on her own. So she took on two apprentices, Rose and Regina. By the time she left Pittsburgh, Shelly had ten employees and rarely left her desk. Taxes were killing her, though. North Dakota promised what she wanted, a chance to expand her business, free from the taxes that spread her wealth around. Rose had come with her, and in two years the business had flourished in Fargo, adding three new employees.

In response to the federal plan to move the military, Mackey and other leaders of FND put out a call for supporters to move to North Dakota. Nationwide, through its state chapters, FND boasted a membership of five million. It was unclear how supportive those members were, though. Some of them may have planned to move to North Dakota after secession, but how willing were they to put skin in the game by moving now?

Tom Pinner had been watching from the sidelines, admiring people who moved to North Dakota and noncommittally planning to go someday himself if secession ever occurred. Like most spectators, he had been amazed by the sheer number of people who had made the move. He had been equally surprised that the federal government had not done anything substantial to stop FND. Now, though, push had come to shove and they were sending in the military. While everyone knew that the feds were just moving in voters, the official rationale was that the troops were there to keep the peace. The insincerity coupled with the armed-guard mentality pushed Tom off the sideline. He wasn't alone.

Just after Tom resolved to go to North Dakota, though, a federal state of emergency was declared. Americans were not permitted to move to North Dakota without federal approval. The administration had invoked executive privilege and declared that as a matter of national security North Dakota was closed. The exception, of course, was necessary military personnel.

FND had to work with what they had, which was half a million voters who had moved to North Dakota plus about twenty-five thousand native North Dakotans who were likely to vote for secession. With those numbers they would lose the referendum to the fifty thousand troops plus the other five hundred and twenty thousand eligible voters, who would vote against secession.

Don blogged that the executive privilege prohibiting immigration and the declaration of a state of emergency were illegitimate. The courts would probably agree, but they were slow to act. FND had very few friends outside its membership ranks, but the federal abuse of power was creating some sympathy. The ACLU filed suit on behalf of Tom Pinner's application for North Dakota citizenship, but he did not get a speedy hearing. He would not have his day in court until after the election.

Aside from the ACLU and some radical groups, there was an uncoordinated conspiracy of silence. While behind closed doors both the political left and the political right agreed that prohibiting Americans from moving to North Dakota was an unjustifiable overreach of federal power, in public they said nothing. The news media simply parroted the administration's talking points. To the public at large, it appeared that the federal government was doing what it had to do to protect the sanctity of the Union. In particular, the administration depicted itself as protecting the people of North Dakota. Their state had been co-opted by fringe radicals who wanted to secede from the United States. Up to a point, FND's plans and activities had been tolerated as free speech and assembly. The people of North Dakota had a right to their state, though, and it was time for the federal government to intervene and give it back to them.

Mackey called for peaceful confrontation with the military occupation, but not everyone agreed that nonviolence was the answer. Charlie Foreman had begun to assemble and train a militia. It was ragtag, to be sure, and laughable considering that its opposition was the United States Army. But that was not the point. They would not face the Army on a battlefield. Instead, they would make life difficult and precarious for them, picking off individual members in convoys and drawing them into a fight. Foreman's men were more than willing to be martyrs; some even volunteered unsolicited to act as suicide bombers to take out a military base. Mackey knew no good could come of it.

On the radio John Lennon sang about Chairman Mao. Mackey brought Foreman his meatloaf and mashed potatoes and sat down across from him in the booth. "Please, Charlie. I know you're angry. I'm angry too. But this isn't the way to go."

Foreman tucked his napkin into the open collar of his red and black flannel shirt. "What are we supposed to do, Mack? Sit back and take it? Let them occupy our land and subvert our election?"

"Militia can't be the answer, Charlie. Not now. We'll only get our people killed, and we'll lose the public-relations war."

With his mouth full, Foreman responded, "When the people see and read that the U.S. Army has shot and killed American citizens, they'll take our side."

Mackey stretched and leaned back. "That might happen if the Army shot non-combatants, peaceful people making speeches and lining up to vote. But you know how the administration and the media are going to portray your men. You'll be depicted as a bunch of gun-toting yahoos who want to do the unthinkable, break away from the United States."

"I can't help the way they'll depict us."

"But you can. Hold off on things."

Wiping his mouth Foreman said, "We have no immediate plans for action, but I can't promise you anything, Mack."

Leaning in, Mackey entreated, "Promise me you'll hold off until after the convention. Give us a chance to present ourselves to the world as wanting to peacefully withdraw from the United States. Let us try to make things happen that way."

"All right, Mack. You have until after the convention. No promises after that. Maybe we can even arrange for the U.S. Army to shoot someone peaceful like you suggest."

"That wasn't my suggestion. Besides, how would you do that?"

"Don't worry about it, Mack. Things can be done. How about bringing me some of that apple pie Mary makes?"

Without a word, Mackey slid out of the booth.

The convention was scheduled for September 16 in Bismarck, the state capital. Lorna had taken the lead in organizing events and coordinating with local FND groups and lone wolves throughout the state. The quiet revolution would need to get noisy to show the world what it was about. Originally, the convention was going to be a pep rally for the FND faithful, but now the convention had to be a public-relations infomercial that would put the Free North Dakota movement in a sympathetic light. Lorna was working overtime, changing and rearranging speakers and ceremonies. She had always known that conditions could and probably would change so that the plans couldn't be written in stone. But she hadn't anticipated that there would be an occupying army that would outnumber them at the voting booth.

Lying in bed next to Don, Lorna said, "I'm in over my head."

Without rolling over to face her, he said, "We all are."

"But I'm the one planning this convention. And it's not just a ra-ra pep rally anymore."

"Ahh, don't start with that."

"With what?"

"You can get the job done."

"But what is the job, Don? Right now it looks like one thing, but that may change six times before September 16. And the people I have to work with aren't exactly team players by nature."

"Yeah, it's a tough situation."

"Why did I let you and Mackey get me into this?"

Don turned to face her saying, "You know we didn't get you into anything. No one made you take that apron. I was perfectly happy playing that role. You know that you only do what you want to do. And you know you want to do this."

\* \* \*

The Pentagon's plan was in full swing. Ten thousand troops had already been relocated to North Dakota by April. The rest would come incrementally through the summer, with the last of them arriving in September. Risk analysis gave the plan a 97% chance of success. But of course the Pentagon had also predicted that U.S. troops would be greeted as liberators in Iraq and that the mission in Afghanistan would be completed in a timely manner.

There were some skeptics behind closed doors, but in public there was nothing but confidence, both in reports to the White House and to the media, concerning Mission North Dakota. The logistics of moving the troops were a nightmare, but morale was high.

# 21

Since no combat was anticipated, Sarah felt a bit silly going to North Dakota as a nurse with her reserve unit. With fifty thousand troops gathered in close proximity, there would be demand for basic medical care, though. At least the mission would be short and well-defined, a cakewalk compared to a tour of duty in Iraq. Ben was annoyed by the whole thing, mostly just for selfish reasons—he didn't want to be without Sarah. But like the rest of the country he was supportive of the mission. He had first heard about Free North Dakota on CNN three years ago. They had interviewed some guy saying they hoped to attract half a million people to North Dakota who wanted to secede and form their own libertarian nation. Like most people outside of North Dakota, Ben lost track of the story at that point. The news media had more urgent stories to cover with the war in Kashmir and the Israeli-Palestinian conflict in addition to the impeachment of the Speaker of the House on charges of accepting corporate bribes.

Like most Americans, Ben knew the terms "liberal" and "conservative," which had become practically synonymous with "Democrat" and "Republican," but he had no idea what a libertarian was until he Googled it. Libertarian, it turned out, meant being more liberal than most liberals on social issues, like drugs and prostitution, and more conservative than most conservatives on economic issues like taxes and entitlement programs. What sense did that make? Well, when you thought about it, it made a lot of sense. It was consistent on the value of liberty. The liberal Democrats wanted liberty on social issues like drugs, marriage rights, and abortion, but they did not want liberty on economic issues. They did not recognize property rights as being on par with other basic rights like freedom of speech, assembly, and religion. Instead they believed in redistribution, spreading the wealth around. By contrast, the conservative Republicans were better on economic liberty, though even they weren't very good, still allowing for a lot of redistribution to fund the welfare state. But the Republicans were awful on liberty when it came to social issues.

As Ben read more and dug deeper, he discovered the frustration that the Free North Dakota movement felt with the entrenched two-party system and their inability to get their voice heard. They wanted to have an experiment in democracy, a chance to have a society based on their philosophy, which they considered to be in the spirit of the original American democracy. In principle Free North Dakota supported other secession movements around the world, like the Quebecois in Canada and the Catalan in Spain. From reading Don Jenkins's *Soda Blog*, Ben gathered that Free North Dakota had some connections to the Second Vermont Republic, a quasi-socialist secession movement. *"We won't know what works best and for whom until we try,"* Don blogged.

Ben had never been very political; he just liked to be left alone. He figured government was a necessary evil; we need it to do a lot of things. As long as government didn't show up too much in his daily life, as long as it mostly left him alone, that was fine. He had grown uncomfortable with the extent to which government was becoming involved in the healthcare system; he wasn't sure who was worse, the government or the insurance companies. Either way, he was buried in paperwork.

It seemed like things must have been better a generation or two ago, but maybe not. The problem with the healthcare system, as Ben saw it, was that no one was paying for themselves and so no one knew what anything cost. All of his patients had some form of insurance, which they paid for dearly through their employers in the form of decreased salary. And as long as care was covered by insurance, they didn't exercise any discrimination, didn't know or care what things cost. By contrast, when it came to procedures that were not covered by insurance, like

LASIK eye surgery and cosmetic surgery, patients were very cost conscious. The result was that doctors competed for their business, and prices had gone down while the quality of care had gone up. Under the current system, medical insurance covered practically everything, from routine office visits to major surgery. But imagine what would happen if car insurance covered gasoline, oil changes, and flat tires. If people weren't paying for those things themselves, the prices would go up. Ben had come to think that medical insurance should only cover catastrophic cases, surgery and hospitalization, the kind of things that are major financial burdens. That would keep the cost of healthcare down. Of course you still want people to get regular check ups and come to the doctor when they're sick and take the medicine that they're prescribed. But people would have more money in their pockets if insurance covered less and cost less, and they would be more willing to pay for those services if they cost less. This all just made sense. But try to do anything about it and you'd be discouraged before you ever got started.

The government and insurance-company bureaucracies were firmly entrenched and were skilled at preserving themselves. Plus, there was no public will to change things except to make them worse, to make people even more dependent on government and insurance. Ben had been aware of all of the healthcare issues for a while, but his life was easy and comfortable. He certainly wasn't going to spend his personal time and energy lobbying for changes that would never come.

Like most people, Ben had assumed that the problems were largely confined to his own area of business. In other areas, government intervention was good and necessary. From the outside, it always looks like government regulation is necessary to keep power in check and protect the little people. But from the inside it's clear that, although well intended, government regulation is poorly informed and ends up hurting the people it is intended to protect through unintended consequences. It always hurts the little guy by making the cost of compliance in terms of dollars, time, and energy burdensome and, in some cases, prohibitive. It's the big, established companies that succeed and benefit by the way regulation kills off competition from smaller, emerging firms.

The more Ben looked into it, the more he became convinced, and the less happy he was with Sarah's deployment to North Dakota. Not only would he be missing his wife for several months, but she would be serving to stop an exercise in freedom, an experiment that just might work. Of course it might not work for everyone, but, as Don Jenkins argued on the *Soda Blog*, that was the point. No one would be compelled to be a part of it. Current residents of North Dakota could retain their U.S. citizenship or move to the U.S. People from the Second Vermont Republic would not be flocking to North Dakota. They had their own sort-of-socialist view of what would be best, and they were welcome to try it. Who knows? It might work out well for them.

At first, Ben was hesitant to say anything to Sarah. He knew it was hard enough on her being away, and he knew she believed in the mission. But after a few weeks he began to raise the subject in phone conversation.

"Have you had much contact with the Free North Dakota people?"

"No, we just stay in camp. You know that. It's boring."

"I've been reading about them online. Some of their ideas make sense."

"Like what?"

Ben shifted in his seat. "Well, they want government out of the healthcare business. Basically, they want liberty, freedom."

"That's all well and good, Ben, but not everyone can handle freedom."

Pushed back by Sarah's impatient response, Ben asked, "But shouldn't we all be held responsible for our free choices and their consequences at a certain point?"

"In theory, yes, but in practice lots of people never grow up. They need to be taken care of."

Pleading, Ben asked, "But who is obligated to take care of them?" Before Sarah could respond, he continued, "These FND people are saying that they don't want to be compelled to take care of other people and they don't want the government to make them take care of them."

"That's nice, Ben. But they can't just seize North Dakota and leave the Union. They're free to leave and go to another country or buy a desert island somewhere, so let them do that."

Ben dropped the subject and just told Sarah how much he missed her. He really did. Pictures of Sarah did her no justice; she was far from photogenic. What made her attractive was the sparkle in her eye, the curve of her smile—the kinds of things that you had to see in motion, things that couldn't be captured and frozen in a photograph. And it was her company that he missed. The phone was fine, but he missed the spontaneous interactions that the phone didn't allow for, the cuddles, the nuzzles, the light flirtations, the time on the couch watching TV in the evening, feeling her twitch just before she fell asleep at night. Without Sarah to fill his hours, Ben began reading more about libertarianism.

The more Ben read, the more he liked what FND was trying to achieve. It was a pity that they had no chance of success at this point. Maybe they would have been better off finding an island somewhere. Maybe that's what they would do after the election in November. Over half a million of them had moved to North Dakota, and there wasn't much in North Dakota to keep them after the election. Of course they could just stay and put the referendum on the ballot again for the following November, but the federal government would probably break up the group before that, perhaps even charge the leaders with treason.

* * *

Lorna saw them driving in convoys everywhere. The camouflage of the vehicles made them stick out. Mostly they were just Humvees and other transport vehicles. The troops needed something to do and so they were put in motion. These men and women under the American flag did not feel friendly. After 9/11 everyone in a military uniform had begun to look like a hero despite the unheroic deeds of many. There was something surreal, though, about seeing so many of these men and women in uniform moving among you. They always looked like freedom fighters on TV, liberating Iraq and keeping the peace in Afghanistan, but here they looked like alien invaders. The precision with which they moved indicated a lack of conscious thought. These men and women had made themselves into obedient machines, a fact that stood out all the more in the rebellious intellectual landscape of North Dakota. Lorna did not fear the force with which these troops might strike, though that remained an ever-present possibility. She feared them as one might imagine fearing alien space invaders who could not comprehend the value of what they might destroy. So Lorna resolved to reach out, to get to know members of the occupying force, to let them know what she was about and what they were really opposing.

The flag was the obstacle. These occupiers proudly wore and flew the American flag, a symbol that FND had abandoned but not yet replaced. The flag simplified things by shutting down thought. It was sacred and ultimate, and the value of what it stood for could not be questioned. When these men and women in uniform had doubts about a mission in a foreign land they could look to the flag they had pledged allegiance to as children. Even if the particular mission was dubious, it was part of a greater mission in support of the greatest nation on earth, and the flag was the symbol of that nation. The same rationale applied in North Dakota. It seemed like few of the military men and women had any doubts about the value of their mission, and if they did, then all they had to do was look to the flag. It made life like an old western movie in which they were wearing the white hats.

* * *

Roger Varrick drew stares and comments from the crowd at Mackey's Diner, but Lorna saw the opportunity she had been looking for.

Mary Mackey took his order of bacon and eggs, which he ate silently, until Lorna appeared at his booth.

"More coffee, Captain?"

She shimmered. His voice shook. "Yes, ma'am."

"Oh, *ma'am* makes me feel old. Call me Lorna. See, it's on my nametag."

"OK, Lorna, then call me Roger."

"Roger, Roger."

He smiled.

"Ha! So how long have you worked here, Lorna?"

"Oh, a few months."

"So you know a lot about Free North Dakota?"

She touched his hand on the table, saying, "I know a little. One thing I've come to know is that I don't know a lot about anything."

He paused as if to contemplate her words. Really, he was recovering from the electricity of her touch. "Well said."

"Thank you, Roger."

"You don't sound like you're from around here."

"No, I'm from Virginia originally. But I lived in New York for years. I followed my boyfriend three years ago and we never left."

Roger was deflated by the mention of a boyfriend, but he managed to reply, "So you got involved with FND?"

"You could say that."

"Well, what would you say?"

Lorna put the coffeepot on his table and held his gaze. "I don't say much, but I'm expected to give a speech at the convention in September."

"The FND convention in Bismarck?"

"That's right."

"How did that happen?"

"Well, I'm the convention planner, and Mackey and a bunch of other FND people want me to speak."

"Are you pulling my leg, Lorna?"

"No sir."

Roger Varrick left with Lorna's phone number and a giddy high that he hadn't felt since college. It would have been enough if she were just some pretty, flirty waitress. Those eyes had locked him in. Everything they said made him feel that there was more to know. No secrets had been revealed, only depths gestured at. You could sometimes have that experience with a waitress who knew the score, but this was a different order of magnitude. Roger was sure he got more than the usual treatment of expressive eyes and interested questions.

# 22

Sarah spent her time organizing medical supplies that would get no use. On other deployments things were tense even when they were calm. There was an enemy out there; things could and would go wrong. The enemy would attack without warning; lives and limbs would be lost. In North Dakota there was a chance of attack from a militia, but that was highly unlikely. The mission was strange. Despite what the brass said, they were not there to keep the peace. Sarah felt like a drone sent to pull a lever in a voting booth.

The more Sarah spoke with Ben about FND and libertarianism, the less supportive of her mission she became. Forcing the military to come and vote struck her as just the kind of thing FND was reacting against. They were tired of government interference. And what was this military intervention but interference with the will of the people?

On the other hand, Sarah felt sympathy for the people of North Dakota. Only about five percent of them supported secession. They were being hijacked. Many of their families had lived in North Dakota for generations; they saw beauty and value in a land that others scoffed at. Yet they were at risk of becoming strangers, foreigners really, on their own land. This had already occurred to the extent that they had been outnumbered by the FND people. Some natives welcomed this; you couldn't argue with success. There had been lots of growing pains, but in recent years, the North Dakota economy had grown and flourished like never before, and the prospects for the economic future were bright if secession occurred. Most withheld their assent, though. Even if good consequences would follow, they did not appreciate the takeover from outside. North Dakota's Native American population found this hypocritical. The white man had stolen these lands long ago, and now the descendants of invaders considered themselves peaceful natives in need of protection.

Nearly thirty thousand troops had arrived by the Fourth of July. Most North Dakotans celebrated American independence as they always had, with cookouts and fireworks and flags and parades. No one took America for granted this year, though. The flag and the thought of all those who had died for it through the years brought tears to many eyes. The troops were weary from the move, the set up, and the daily drudgery of life in camp, but they too experienced Independence Day on a deeper level than ever before. As the original American patriots had fought to liberate themselves from tyranny, so they would liberate Americans who were threatened by the tyranny of an artificially produced majority. No bullets would need to fly, but their mission would be in the same grand tradition that stretched from the revolutionaries through the Union troops of the Civil War, the D-Day liberators of World War II, and beyond.

The fireworks of the Fourth of July rang ironically in the ears of FND that year, as the cherry bombs and M-80s recalled the musket fire of the ragtag colonial forces opposing the fearsome red coats. The natives and the troops were celebrating satisfaction with themselves as the heirs to that revolution, but they were not the underdogs that the colonists were. Instead, they sat in a position of strength, stopping a revolution, a quiet revolution that aimed to shed no blood, to proceed by democratic vote, and to leave people alone. FND members saw themselves as the genuine heirs of the American Revolution, throwing off a tyrannical government, not destroying it, just demanding release.

\* \* \*

Spending his days alone in the apartment, Don was struggling to write a blog piece on the military presence in North Dakota and the illegitimate and unprecedented government manipulations of the military to preserve federal power. The message was nothing new, but he wanted to convey the strange fear of seeing the American military and feeling not protected but threatened. For the first time Don understood the black community's reaction to the police. *"The police may be there 'to serve and protect' but it doesn't feel like it's you who they're there to serve and protect. You, actually, are suspicious and they are more than ready to run you down."*

Don noted that it's not just blacks who have this reaction to the cops. Most people feel threatened. Cops have the power, and there are so many little laws that you're almost always in violation of at least one. Only rarely does the sight of a uniformed police officer inspire a sense of safety. *"At their best they are unapproachable, like some father or football coach who will be quick to misunderstand you and send you on your way."* Don's experience with the seat-belt ticket had only hardened him against the police. With age it had become easier for him to look at individual cops as the dopey, unaccomplished kids that they are. But, on the more sinister side, Don recalled that the guys he knew growing up who had become cops could easily have gone the other way. In fact, some of them had.

Many cops were ex-military, of course, and the military had a more benevolent appearance. They could not and would not arrest you. Your enemies were their enemies, the real bad guys who were out there in the wide world beyond the nation's borders. But here they were. You were trying to leave and they were making you stay. You had no beef with them, but they had no sympathy for you. *"Although they were really just there to vote, they put on a show by keeping on the move and appearing at a state of military preparedness. They were like some all-star basketball team dunking the ball in warm ups. The game wasn't necessary; they just had to show you what they could do. They were just going to vote, but if things got out of hand they were ready to do more."*

The military undermined the platform on which Don stood, leaving him surrounded by splinters of thoughts and ideas. What had he done by getting so involved with FND and investing so much emotionally? He had taken Lorna away from her life and she had betrayed him by taking his spotlight.

# 23

During the previous year Andyne stock had risen continuously, but in response to the military presence in North Dakota the stock lost all its gains. Lester Naylor was feeling the heat. What could he do about the current state of affairs? "Nothing," was his simple reply to Glen Summers.

"There has to be something," Summers said.

Lester laced his fingers together and placed them on the edge of his desk. "What, Glen? We saw an opportunity and moved on it. For a while it made us look smart, but now we look foolish. That's just the way things go, isn't it?"

Summers sighed. "Ordinarily, Lester, yes. But a lot of important people have a lot of money tied up in Andyne stock and they will not be happy if they lose that money."

Lester unlaced his fingers and turned his palms up. "But they won't lose their money. They'll just lose the gains they made on paper. That's the way the game goes. Any serious investor knows that."

Summers leaned in. "Take my word for it, Lester. It's not as simple as that. There are long tentacles reaching from New York to North Dakota."

"OK, but even so, what can we do about it?"

"We can find a way to make secession go through, Lester." Forming a gun with his thumb and index finger, Summers said, "We need a silver bullet."

\* \* \*

After his first encounter with Lorna, Captain Roger Varrick had become a regular at Mackey's Diner.

Sitting at a booth in the back, he said, "If you want legalized drugs and prostitution and gambling, take it through the legislature."

"If it were that easy, we would," Lorna replied.

"These things take time. Changes don't happen overnight. You have to let them develop and marinate in people's minds."

Lorna sat down and leaned across the table. "But why should we wait? Would you have told black people to wait until society gets around to giving them civil rights?"

"No, of course not. But they protested and took their grievances public. They made people aware and change followed."

Lorna sunk back against the booth. "That's true, Roger, but black people marching for civil rights were sympathetic. FND isn't sympathetic. We're seen as adolescents in the midst of existential rebellion. We want drugs and whores and dice. We want what's ours. We don't want to be taxed to pay for anyone else. We sound selfish and self-centered. There's no chance of succeeding by taking our message to the streets in protest."

Roger raised his eyebrows before taking a sip of his coffee. "Well, maybe there's a reason for that, Lorna."

"What reason is that, Roger?"

"It's the way people see it. It's just the will of the majority."

"But it was the will of the majority that black people and white people should not be able to marry, and it was the will of the majority that two men or two women should not be allowed to marry."

"True."

Lorna put her elbows on the table. "Whenever a majority makes laws that undermine the rights of a minority it's tyranny, tyranny of the majority. Historically it was easy to keep black people down because they had so few votes. Today it's easy to keep us from seceding."

"But if that's the way the majority wants it, Lorna, what more can you say?"

"We can say 'let us go.' If the rest of you want to live by your laws, that's your business, but we want to go. And what we're taking with us is just the most God-forsaken land in the United States."

"But what about the oil, Lorna?"

"You know what? They could even keep the oil. We could yield the most oil-rich parts of North Dakota. That way there would still be a North Dakota in the United States. There would still be fifty stars on the flag. And we could take our Free Dakota and go."

"Well, why don't you propose that to the FND leaders? It would be a good PR move for FND to say they don't want the whole state, they don't even want the oil, they just want a piece of land to call their own."

"That's a good idea, Roger."

"Thanks. Of course it would also relieve worries about the nuclear weapons at the Air Force base in Minot."

"Well, you know, the stated plan has always been to surrender those weapons to the United States, but giving up the whole western part of the state would make that less complicated."

"Right."

Lorna leaned across the table. "So tell me, Roger, how would you vote if we changed things that way?"

"I don't know, Lorna, it would give me reason to think."

"How do you think other members of the military would respond? Would FND look more reasonable or would it look weak?"

"Probably both."

Lorna liked the idea of reshaping the secession to exclude the oil lands in the western part of the state. It would be a demonstration of good faith, and it would make the point that FND just wanted some land to be free and do its own thing. They didn't need a whole state. They wouldn't even use the name North Dakota after secession. The United States would still have its North Dakota, and the new nation would be called Freeland or Free Dakota or something.

Later that day, Lorna told Mackey about the idea to leave the oil-rich parts of the state and just take a smaller slice including Fargo.

"It's a public-relations move," she said.

"How so?"

"Well, the CNN poll says 89% of Americans oppose our secession. Even those who would be unaffected by our secession oppose it because they feel like they would be losing something. They'd lose the feeling of belonging to a Union of fifty states. But if we leave North Dakota and just take part of the land and form our own nation, I'll bet a lot fewer people would object."

Mackey folded his arms as he leaned back against the counter. "That may be right, Lorna, but we're not having a national vote on the issue. We're having a state vote. So what does it matter?"

Lorna stood up. "It's the military that matters. If we can persuade enough of them not to vote against us, then we win. The administration can't compel them to vote against us. So if we can get them to resent the arm-twisting that has deployed them to North Dakota to step in a booth and vote as expected, then we have a chance to win."


Not everyone liked the new idea. Many FND members had relocated to places like Williston and the Bakken oil fields in the hopes of making money in oil, and Andyne was rumored to have almost perfected a new process for extracting oil from shale sand. On the phone from New York Glen Summers said, "This is bad, Lester."

"Bad for who, Glen?"

"Bad for us."

"Who is us?"

"You and me and Andyne."

"Well, it's not optimal, Glen. I agree. But it seems like a good solution, given the circumstances."

"No, it's not. We shouldn't give away too much too soon. We're on the verge of finalizing the shale-oil extraction process. If we could take advantage of that in an environment free of corporate taxes we'd dominate the market."

* * *

Walking from the mess tent after lunch, Sarah took a chance by broaching the subject with Captain Roger Varrick.

"Another day in paradise, Captain."

"How do you mean, Lieutenant?"

"Oh, well, I mean it really is beautiful country, but I wonder about the parts of it we haven't seen. I hear the FND people have some terrific set-ups."

"Would you like to meet some FND folks, Sarah?"

"Certainly, Captain."

"Let's get breakfast tomorrow at 0 600 hours. I know a place that has great pancakes."

"Yes sir."

The next day Captain Roger Varrick came into the diner accompanied by a woman in uniform. Mary Mackey seated them at a booth and Renata took their order. Lorna was late and she had just thrown up in the bathroom. But she snapped to attention when she saw the uniforms and counted the stripes on the on the woman's sleeve. "Good morning, Captain. Good morning, Lieutenant. More coffee?"

"Yes ma'am," they both replied.

"Lorna, this is Lieutenant Sarah Andersen." Roger continued, "Her husband is a member of the FND chapter of Minnesota."

"Terrific. How long has your husband been involved?"

"Just a few months. Actually, it was my deployment that got him involved. He resented my going, and he wanted to find out what the mission was really about. So he started reading about

FND and libertarianism, and he was hooked."

"A lot of people just stumble into this. I know I did. My boyfriend had been involved with a secessionist group in Vermont. Then he was invited out here by Mackey, the guy who owns this diner."

"He's the head of FND, right?"

"Well, there's no head of FND, but Mackey is one of the unofficial leaders."

"Where is he now?"

"In the back making pancakes."

"So, he still cooks at his own diner?"

"Well, being a leader of FND doesn't actually pay the bills, and besides I think Mackey would be here working even if it did."

"Is there any chance I could speak with him?" Sarah asked.

"Probably not today. Things are too busy."

"I'll have to come back then."

"Please do. In the meantime, here's my number. Feel free to call if you'd like to chat."

Sarah texted the next day, and Lorna responded immediately. Hundreds more texts were exchanged until freedom was lost.

# 24

Teddy Roosevelt called it "the strenuous life." As a young man, he had been advised by his doctor against physical exertion, so Teddy went in the opposite direction, reasoning that only exertion could help him against whatever weakness he might have. Teddy took to boxing and developed a fondness for winter skinny dipping in the Potomac. It was a kind of "what doesn't kill you makes you stronger" philosophy. Roosevelt cultivated that mentality during the time he spent in North Dakota, a fact native North Dakotans were tremendously proud of. You didn't see obviously fit and athletic people in Fargo or Bismarck the way you did in Los Angeles or Boulder. But you did see people who subscribed to the philosophy of the strenuous life. The snow runners were the most inspiring to Don.

These were not marathon runners. They weren't even people who looked like they ran. But if you were at your desk before sunrise, the way Don was, you would see them. They ran every day, jogged or trotted really, never in groups, always alone. It would be annoying if they were super-fit, young, and vain. But they weren't. No, the snow runners were always over forty, usually over fifty, and not fit so far as the eye could see. Of course they didn't always run in the snow, but that's only because there wasn't always snow. They always ran, ran every day, and it didn't matter how cold it was or how much snow there was.

It wasn't just about getting exercise. There were safer, easier, more effective ways of getting exercise. These people were challenging themselves by not letting the darkness, the cold, or the snow stop them. Of course they didn't run just because it was cold, dark, and snowy. They continued to run every day even as the mornings grew light, warm, and dry. The mornings remained early, and that was part of the challenge, to run while most people were still asleep in bed. The challenge was to do it every day no matter what, to set oneself a task and rise to meet the challenge. They had already won a victory before the day had even begun. Nothing else could lay a glove on them after that. At least that's how Don felt just watching them out the window.

He'd be at his desk drinking Metamucil and trying to write a post for his blog, and he'd catch them out of the corner of his eye. There were three in particular, who he saw at the same times every day. He wasn't looking for them, but like the tolling of church bells, they would come and they would validate his efforts. The saying has it that the race is not always for the swift but for those who keep running. While old high-school track stars and former marathoners slept late and told themselves they couldn't face starting to run again because it would mean starting slow, the snow runners kept going. There was no finish line, there was no clock, there was just the run.

Sitting up in bed with a rerun of *Law and Order* on TV, Lorna asked Don, "Why are you so obsessed with them?"

"Part of it is that they do it alone," he said. "Running is a lot easier when you do it with someone else. A partner can help you commit to a time and place and distance. And then while you're running, a partner can make the time pass with conversation. It's a balancing act to talk while running, to get the pace right so that you're able to keep your breath and talk at the same time. That, in addition to the conversation, takes up a lot of focus. You get absorbed in the conversation, and so the time passes quickly."

"But that's a good thing, isn't it?"

Turning over to face her, Don replied, "Nothing wrong with it. But these people run solo. They might like to have a partner, but somehow I doubt it. The extra exertion, the extra challenge of going it alone is part of the appeal for them."

"But why make life harder for yourself?"

Sitting up now, Don replied, "That's exactly the point. Life is hard, so the paradoxical solution is to make it harder. When you impose a challenge on yourself first thing in the morning and you overcome that challenge, then every other challenge you meet through the course of the day appears that much more manageable. These people are shot full of endorphins after their runs. Their brain chemistry is telling them that they're winners, that they have survived a challenge."

"Yeah, I get that, but it has to be lonely out there in the dark and the cold. Why not go to a gym and run on a treadmill? I've always found that the energy of a gym makes me work harder."

"It's true. They could probably run faster and longer if they got on a treadmill and let the energy of a gym spur them along. And that wouldn't be cheating. It would just be losing."

"Losing what, Don? It's not a competition."

"Right. I don't mean losing as opposed to winning. I mean losing as opposed to gaining. Outside they gain from the fresh air and the scenery and the chance to observe the subtleties of nature and the gradual shifting of the seasons. The rest of us fight nature by locking ourselves inside. The snow runners fight nature by embracing it."

"Well, at least they have music to move them along."

Don muted the television. "No, Lorna, no iPods. You know why?"

"Safety?"

"No, it's not the safety issue. Sure, lots of serious runners forgo iPods because they're afraid of being hit by a car. But the snow runners don't want to miss the sounds. It's amazing how quiet it is before dawn, but there are little sounds of the world waking. And those sounds change with the seasons. The winter is quiet. That's the thing about it. You can see winter, but you can't hear it. Or really, it has the sound of silence. No smell either. Fall smells of dying leaves, but gradually that smell disappears and you're left with nothing. Occasionally you may smell the smoke from a wood-burning stove, but that's fleeting. Most of the time winter smells of nothing, which makes life all the more glorious when the smells of spring return."

Lorna smirked and squinted with one eye. "Wow, Don. You've thought a lot about this. But since you're just sitting there at your computer in the morning, how do you know?"

"I've run with them in my mind."

"Oh come on." Lorna pushed him gently with one hand.

"No, seriously. I'm a writer. It's good for a writer to write about what he knows, but you can't restrict yourself to just that. You have to be able to stretch things to places you've never been and experiences you've never had."

"So you could be wrong."

"Sure, I could be wrong factually, but even if I am, I'm still right about what I've imagined—that things could be that way. And that's what really matters."

"All right, then, continue, Mr. Writer."

"So running through winter is running through death towards the resurrection of spring when the earth comes alive again, not just with the sights of green grass and leaves but with the sounds of birds and the smells of earth."

"Now you're going off the deep end. Besides, if you're using your imagination to conjure all of this, why don't the runners do the same thing? Why not just run on a treadmill with eyes closed and imagination open?"

Don hugged her tight. "Feel that? There's no resistance on a treadmill. You can program the treadmill to simulate a hill or to go faster, but the surface is always equally smooth. For the snow runners, part of the challenge is the surface. Running on top of packed snow is a bit like running on the beach. You sink into the snow like you sink into the sand. Your step doesn't bounce back the way it does on the springy surface of the treadmill."

Don released her and she fell back on her pillow with a laugh.

"So it's about making things harder for yourself, the 'strenuous life' thing?"

"That's part of it, but it's also about the experience. In addition to the cold on the skin, the experience of the snow resisting your steps, trying to suck you in, is another sensory experience."

"So it's all sensory?" she said, sitting up.

"No, a lot of it is mental. You have to put your feet in the right place with every stride, avoiding icy patches. And that makes the run on the same route different every day. It's easy to slip and fall or twist an ankle. So it takes concentration to make the right decisions for foot placement at a moment's notice. That's another reason they don't wear iPods. The task is absorbing enough, and without proper concentration they would get hurt."

"Sounds like *Tetris* again, Don."

"That's right. Things come down at you, and you don't get to choose what they are. But you do get to choose how to arrange them to make it all work. The running is absorbing the way *Tetris* is, demanding all your attention."

"If that's right, Don, then it's like a form of meditation, or at least right mindfulness."

"What do you mean?"

"Buddhism calls for right mindfulness, focusing your attention completely on the task at hand. So some monks will chop wood or wash dishes repeatedly to cultivate right mindfulness with the goal of bringing that kind of focus into the rest of their life. And right mindfulness is a prelude to right concentration, which is also called meditation, focusing your mind on nothing at all except maybe your breath or a mantra."

"I'll buy that. Sometimes I've thought of the snow runners as in a kind of a trance, but maybe it's more like meditation. Maybe some people even achieve that on a treadmill, but it's hard for me to see it that way. When I see those people in neat rows in their sleek running clothes on those machines, I can't help but think of them as feeding the machines rather than being fed by them. Some may close their eyes and imagine that they're going somewhere, but I doubt that most of them do. Most of them are reading the crawl at the bottom of CNN, while listening to electronic music on their iPods, and bouncing unnaturally off the rubbery surface."

"They're not going anywhere."

"That's right, Lorna. They've removed the purpose from their activity. They just want the byproducts. They want to burn calories and release endorphins. They succeed but without a sense of what they lose. It's like masturbating, you get the same release but something is missing."

"True. There's no substitute for actual sex. It has a purpose, and I don't mean making babies," she said with a twinge. Lorna had no intention of conceiving when she stopped taking the pill. In fact, she hadn't considered it a genuine possibility at her age.

"Yeah, that's part of the problem with prostitutes. At first it's exciting to be with a flesh-and-blood person, but it becomes like jerking off into another person. At first I tried to remedy that by changing girls every time, but then I found that didn't work because the impersonal experience was always the same. That's when I got monogamous with Casey."

*Should I tell him?* she thought to herself. Lorna had seen been shocked to see Casey at the gym. Afterwards they had lunch and Casey told her that she had set up shop as a dominatrix in Fargo. Lured by Mackey and FND, she had decided to take control. Don still had no idea. No, this was not the time to tell him.

Lorna continued, "It's a tightrope walk for a prostitute. We want to build a connection with clients so that they keep coming back, but we can't afford to get emotionally invested ourselves. If I read your snow runners metaphor right, though, it's a validation for monogamy."

Don sat up a little and ran his fingers through his thick gray hair. "I hadn't thought of it that way. They run by themselves, not with a partner."

Lorna sat up cross-legged in bed. "Think of it this way, Don. You run the same route every day, no matter what the weather, and you find ways to appreciate the subtle changes that make the same route always different. It's a difficult commitment, but it's rewarding. You don't march towards death, you make love to the run."

Don smiled and took Lorna's hands in his. "For better or worse."

"'Til death do us part."

"So what do you think, Lorna?"

"What do you mean, what do I think?"

Don got out of bed and got down on one knee. "Let's get married. Will you marry me, Lorna?"

Lorna got out of bed. "Get off the ground. Where is this coming from?"

Don stood up. "It all just made sense right now. I know I've been jealous ever since you replaced me at the diner, but I can't imagine life without you."

"This isn't some *Tetris* game, Don. You're not stuck with the pieces that fall from the sky. You can get rid of them and start over. You can imagine something different."

"You're the one I want."

Lorna shook her head. "There's another piece you don't know about, Don."

"What are you talking about?"

"I'm pregnant."

Don shuddered. "When were you going to tell me?"

"When I made up my mind about whether to keep it."

# 25

When Colonel Abrams called Sarah and Roger into his office, they knew they were not going to be congratulated for taking the initiative in reaching out to FND.

"Captain, Lieutenant, I understand that you have been frequenting Mackey's Diner in Akston."

"Yes sir," said Roger.

"Great pancakes," added Sarah with a nervous laugh.

Abrams scowled. "So am I to believe that you drive all that way just because you like the pancakes?"

"No sir."

"No sir."

"So why, then, do you visit this diner?"

Roger shifted in his seat. "Well, sir, if I may be permitted to speak for the lieutenant as well…"

"Yes, continue."

"We're interested in learning more about FND, and this diner is a center of FND activity."

"You are aware, aren't you, that our mission is to keep the peace between FND and the other citizens of North Dakota?"

"Yes sir."

"That we ourselves are eligible to vote in the North Dakota state election?"

"Yes sir."

"And you are aware that we remain members of the United States Army as well?"

"Yes sir."

"And therefore that any action that subverts the chain of command is subject to court martial?"

"Yes sir."

"Good, then I am ordering you to stay out of Mackey's Diner."

"Is that understood?"

"Yes sir."

"Yes sir."

"And I do not wish to have conversations like, or related to, this one in the future. Is that clear?"

"Yes sir."

"Yes sir."

"Very good. Dismissed."

With a crisp salute and an about face, Roger and Sarah exited Colonel Abrams' office and proceeded to duty at the camp. Sarah texted Lorna immediately. Only later, behind the mess tent, did she have a chance to speak freely with Roger. They stood just beyond a group of smokers not looking at one another.

"What did that mean, Roger?"

"It means they're watching us and the game is over."

"What game? This isn't a game, Roger."

"It was all well and good for us to look into FND and sympathize a bit, but now we've been ordered to cease and desist."

"The colonel's order was just to stay out of Mackey's Diner. We can still…"

Roger interrupted, "His message was clear: stay away from FND or face court martial."

Sarah turned to face him. "Could he really do that? Court martial us for fraternizing with a political group?"

Roger looked away. "We've been given an order, and if we disobey the order then we can be found guilty of insubordination."

"But technically the order was just to stay out of the diner."

Roger looked her in the eye for the first time. "Sarah, as your friend and as a superior officer, I'm telling you to give it up."

"That's it then, Roger? You're going to compromise your principles just because the colonel gave you an order? Isn't that letting yourself be bullied the way that FND is being bullied?"

"That's it, Sarah, it's over."

Sarah texted Lorna and then called her husband, believing that the line wasn't being tapped, at least not yet. "Guess what, honey?"

"What?"

"Guess who's been banned from Mackey's Diner?"

"What did you do?"

"Nothing."

"You must have done something to piss off FND. Why did they ban you?"

"Oh, *they* didn't."

"Then who did?"

"The military, my commander—Colonel Abrams."

"What? Why?"

"He didn't give a reason, but the reason was clear: we're not here to help FND."

"Can they really stop you?"

"Captain Varrick says they can, that they can court martial me for insubordination."

"Then you better not do anything more, Sarah. It's not worth it."

"What do you mean it's not worth it? Of course I have to do something."

"Think about it, Sarah. What can you really do? Nothing much, and the cost of doing nothing much is a court martial. Do the cost-benefit analysis. It's just not worth it."

"There has to be something I can do that will make it worth it."

"Sarah, don't be foolish. In a couple of months this will all be over. I want you home safe and sound. I miss you."

"I miss you too."

The signatures had been gathered and the referendum had been officially amended. The territory that would secede excluded all the oil-rich lands in the western part of the state. Ultimately it was only about one third of the land mass of North Dakota that would secede. The amended referendum did not increase support for FND, however. So Sarah did the only thing she could think of doing.

She texted Lorna to let her know she was on her way. The only chance for secession at this point was if massive numbers of the military took the side of FND and either voted for secession or just abstained on the referendum. How to make that happen was the mystery. Surely, there were others among the military like Sarah and Roger who supported FND, but their numbers were small and would need to increase exponentially.

Sarah arrived at the diner harried from the drive and sweating from the unseasonable September heat. The place was nearly empty, but there was no sign of Lorna. Then she pushed through the swinging doors from the kitchen, a small bump starting to show. After some chatter with a couple of regulars at the counter Lorna made her way to Sarah's booth. Sarah stood and they embraced.

"You look upset. What's going on? Your texts were so cryptic. Where's the captain?"

"I am upset."

"You're shaking. Let's sit."

"He's back at camp. You won't be seeing him anymore."

"Why not?"

"We've been ordered not to come here."

Lorna reached across the table and held Sarah's hands. "Because of FND?"

"Not in so many words, but yes."

"Can they do that?"

"I didn't think so, but apparently they can. An order is an order in the military. They can lock me up for insubordination."

Lorna looked her in the eye. "So why are you here, sweetie? We could have talked on the phone."

"Because we have an opportunity..."

\* \* \*

Losing the shale-oil sands meant a decline in Andyne stock. Lester was ready to pack up and return to New York when Summers called.

"You have to finish what you started, Lester."

"It is finished, and we lost."

"It looks that way, but you don't want to be one of those people who leaves the game early to beat the traffic and then has to listen to the comeback on the car radio."

"You think there's going to be comeback?"

"No, I don't think so."

"Then what are you talking about, Glen?"

"I'm talking about seeing things through to the end, about being the fan who sits in his nose-bleed seat enduring the cold even when the players on the field have given up."

"Isn't that just stupid?"

"No, that's loyal, Lester."

"But who would I be loyal to? FND? They've never asked for my loyalty."

"No, it's being loyal to yourself and what you believe in. Besides, there's a lot of work left to do, and if you leave now others will follow. You set up the office; you started the program. No one there wants to stay in North Dakota if secession doesn't go through, but you owe it to them and to yourself to stay and vote, even if that seems symbolic at best."

Lester hung up the phone and nodded.

# 26

There wasn't much for the feds to do. Foreman and his militia hinted at some kind of action, but for the moment none of it passed the bullshit test. The only thing that made sense was that they might try to draw the Army into a fight at their compound, make a stand, put up a resistance, try to make the Army look like the bad guys. But how would they do that? The militia was too small, and its compound was too remote to warrant attention from the Army.

Media were coming into Bismarck from all over the United States and all over the world to cover the convention. FND people drove in from all parts of the state, and many flew in from other states. Hotels were filled to capacity, and the homes of FND members overflowed with out-of-state guests. Lorna had just visited Shelly Robinson, The Pink Plunger, who was hosting a large contingent from Pittsburgh.

Months of planning had come down to this. The convention was a show, not for FND supporters, but for the whole country. The people of the United States had to be convinced to let them go if the referendum passed. That had been the plan for the convention from the start, but now there was another more immediate goal. FND needed votes, and the only people who could give those votes were the military. Of course you didn't just want to pander, but you had to appeal to them.

Lorna hadn't given a speech since law school, yet everyone had presumed she would be a natural at it. Don was at her disposal for the writing, but she wanted to do it herself. The task had haunted her ever since she accepted it, and she had spent countless hours procrastinating, working on other things related to the convention. Now the convention had begun and she still didn't have a speech. The first major speakers would be FND firebrands who would whip up the crowd with cries for freedom and declarations of righteous indignation at the military occupation. That would not be her approach. Don and Mackey wanted her to sell herself, to become the face of the movement.

The media had descended upon the diner with the plan of interviewing the man behind the movement, but they did not find a garrulous leader, eager to oblige them with sound bites. Instead they found a fry cook, who would only shrug and say, "The movement speaks for itself. There's nothing I could tell you that would compare with the fact that more than half a million voters have moved to North Dakota with the hope of being free."

Lorna had taken a few days off from the diner to work on her speech, but she wasn't making any progress. Don's advice was to go back to work. She often had ideas pouring coffee and joking with the regulars. So that's what she did, and while pouring a refill for Josh Weinberg, she realized it wasn't about her at all. She had been fretting because she felt the pressure of the spotlight. But her job was to serve and to put the spotlight on someone else.

Two days later she stood at the podium in front of a capacity crowd at the Bismarck Civic Center.

"I'm here to tell you about a woman who has been taken from us, a reluctant warrior named Sarah Andersen. She did not move to North Dakota to find freedom. She was moved to North Dakota to oppose freedom. It was inconvenient. Sarah is a nurse married to a doctor. They had a quiet life together in St. Paul, Minnesota. But Sarah is also in the Army Reserve. So when the administration gave the order to move the military into North Dakota, Sarah was among the troops mobilized. Like many of you at home, like me, Sarah did not think much about politics. Her life was full enough without worrying about Washington. She loved her country even though she knew it wasn't perfect. When her country called on her to go to North Dakota she wasn't anxious to answer the call, but she was willing. It seemed unreasonable that in this day and age a state would want to secede from the Union.

It would be easy duty. No one said it, but all she was expected to do was show up and vote against secession. No one was telling her how to vote or even telling her *to* vote; they were just expecting her to do as expected. Sarah's husband Ben, resenting his wife's absence, began looking into the Free North Dakota movement, and to his surprise found that he sympathized. Like all Americans, Ben loves liberty. And the more he looked into it, the more he realized that our basic liberties are being compromised. He talked with Sarah, and she began looking into FND herself. Sarah and her commanding officer, Captain Roger Varrick, began coming to Mackey's Diner.

I got to know them there. Sarah and I were fast friends, talking and texting several times a day. She was the first person I told when I realized I was pregnant. I hoped that Sarah and Roger would help spread the word about FND among the military. But the chances of that came to an end on September 12 when Sarah came to the diner without Roger and told me she had been ordered not to come to the diner again. Roger had followed orders and stayed at the camp, but here she was in defiance of orders.

You can guess what happened next. I have not seen her since. Her husband Ben has been unable to speak with her; he doesn't even know her location. She has been detained and is subject to court martial for insubordination because she knowingly disobeyed a direct order from a superior officer.

Following commands is important in the military. It saves lives. There can be no doubt about that. But what was the command in this case? To stay out of a diner? Sarah has taken on our burden. She is you. She is me. She is North Dakota. Let her go. Let her go."

Abruptly Lorna left the stage. The crowd began to chant, "Let her go. Let her go." By the next day the speech had gone viral on the internet, and people were selling t-shirts with Sarah's face framed by the outline of North Dakota and embossed with the slogan "Let her go." The military's official response was to say that there was more to the matter than the public was aware of and that Lieutenant Sarah Andersen was being detained at a base in North Dakota awaiting court martial.

Public support for the military intervention in North Dakota had been extremely high, but no one liked the idea of compelling a soldier to stay out of a diner simply because she was sympathetic to a political cause. Everyone knew the military was there to vote, even though the official rhetoric said they were there to keep the peace. Americans were supportive of the plan, since voting was an effective way to keep the peace. But no one liked the idea that individual soldiers would be compelled to vote a certain way or be prohibited from interacting with FND.

The next day the military doubled down on Sarah's detainment. A spokesman explained that FND was a traitorous organization, and Sarah's fraternization, in violation of a direct order, was therefore treasonous. There were good reasons that her commander ordered her to stay out of the diner, and her disobedience had compromised national security.

This explanation satisfied some people, those who trusted that there is always more to the story than the government is able to tell us, that secrets need to be kept for the sake of security. Apparently, this woman, this nurse-soldier had crossed a line. We would have to trust that the government and the military were dealing with her appropriately in the interest of national security.

Spontaneous demonstrations took shape in Brooklyn, San Francisco, and Seattle. Protesters used the "Let her go" chant, but their t-shirts and posters lacked the image of North Dakota. As far as they were concerned, it was a free-speech issue. As long as Sarah was not on duty, she had the right to speak to whomever, and about whatever, she wanted. The news cycle was slow and uncluttered, so the protests got non-stop coverage.

Lorna was the instant celebrity Mackey knew she would be. At first, the media wanted to talk to her about Sarah and their friendship. Lorna was glad to oblige, but soon enough Lorna herself became the focus of interest. The camera was kind to her. She made the primped and polished women who interviewed her look whorish by comparison. Her story was odd and compelling. Lorna had been raised in a strict evangelical home, rebelled by going to NYU for college, and dropped out of law school to become a high-priced call girl and madam. Years later she fell in love with one of her clients and became interested in a secession movement in Vermont before moving to North Dakota to support secession there. Now she was pregnant and engaged. You couldn't make this stuff up, yet it all seemed so natural and matter of fact to Lorna. She was not putting on airs or making speeches or giving talking points. If an interviewer wanted to spend the whole time talking about her experience as a madam, Lorna was glad to talk about it. The public couldn't get enough, couldn't stop watching.

\* \* \*

At Andyne, hopes were high once again that secession was a genuine possibility. Summers congratulated himself for staying in the game and convincing Lester to do the same. "It ain't over 'til it's over," Summers said.

"Yogi Berra?"

"That's right, Lester, the dugout sage."

"But, Glen, doesn't this just prolong the inevitable? We're still not going to win the referendum."

"Not if the vote was taken tomorrow, but we have time. Things can happen."

"What things?"

"People love Lorna."

"They may love her, Glen, but that's not going to make the

military vote with us."

"We'll see."

* * *

"On your knees, bitch boy."

"Yes, mistress."

"So you think you can manipulate Lorna? Get her to do what you want?"

"No, mistress."

Casey took off her leather glove and smacked Summers's face. "Don't lie to me."

* * *

The appetite for Lorna was insatiable. It had started with cable-news interviews, but it had spread to every corner of the enter-tainment industry. *The National Enquirer* and other gossip magazines had been the first to jump on board with salacious headlines implying a lesbian relationship between Lorna and Sarah. Glad for the publicity, Lorna said they were just friends, that she had slept with women in the past but that she didn't find Sarah attractive in that way. Asked whether the feeling was mutual, Lorna replied that she couldn't speak for Sarah. That was enough to spark the national libido.

Sarah's husband Ben didn't appreciate Lorna's implication, but at least she was bringing attention to the injustice. Now the media were talking to Ben too, but mostly they wanted to know about Sarah's relationship with Lorna and FND. Interviewers were disappointed when they couldn't get him to say a negative word. He supported FND and secession. Didn't he blame Lorna for getting Sarah in over her head? No, Sarah knew what she was doing. Had he heard from Sarah? No, she was being detained in an undisclosed location, and his attempts to contact her had been unsuccessful. Ben was cool. He understood that the longer Sarah stayed in detention, the better it was for FND. That was what Sarah wanted. Though it pained him to think of her as a prisoner, Ben was proud of his wife.

\* \* \*

The guy wore a batting helmet all the time. No, Leon didn't play ball. He just wore the batting helmet the way other guys wore a baseball cap. At first you might think he wore it because of the rain. When didn't it rain in Seattle? Water rolled right off the batting helmet, unlike a hat that would absorb it. But he wore the batting helmet on sunny days too. So maybe it was just force of habit developed from all those rainy days. Maybe, but it was still odd. It was a Yankees batting helmet with a Dellwood Milk insignia on the back, a cheap give-away from "batting helmet day" at Yankee Stadium some time back in the early '80s. The helmet was a bit of a collector's item at this point, though probably not worth much in its current condition. Seattle and the protesters didn't care for the Yankees, but Leon made no apologies. He just wore the helmet. Occasionally, someone would ask him why he wore a batting helmet, but he had no answer, just thought the question was strange. He liked it, so why wouldn't he wear it?

Front and center at the protests in Seattle with a bullhorn in hand, Leon had become a celebrity. You could pick him out in every photo and video clip. Bloggers took to calling him "batting-helmet boy." It was condescending and seemed to imply that he might be slightly retarded, but it was apt. Batting-helmet boy was outraged at the detainment of Sarah Andersen. Her first-amendment rights had been violated and she was being held illegally. It was batting-helmet boy who suggested that Sarah was imprisoned at Guantanamo Bay—that was why no one had seen her. Of course, he had no basis for this claim, but the sound bite of him saying it had gone viral. The military actually responded. They denied that Sarah was being held at Guantanamo and reiterated that she was being held at an undisclosed location in North Dakota. The media asked batting-helmet boy for his response. "That's easy for them to say. Show me the money. Show me Sarah." The crowd behind him began to chant it, "Show me Sarah. Show me Sarah. Show me Sarah."

The military knew they were losing the public-relations war, but they weren't going to dignify the dictates of a jobless moron in a batting helmet. So the conspiracy stories grew. Of course, for the most part, the general public recognized the stories as bullshit. Sarah was not being tortured in some secret lair in Guantanamo. But the military's refusal to show Sarah to the public made the military look even more unreasonable. Why didn't they just leave this poor girl alone? Yes, she seemed like a girl to most Americans with her innocent eyes and bobbed hair. It was hard to think of Sarah as a woman when she was juxtaposed with Lorna. The sympathy worked both ways for Sarah, though. Of course she really was a woman, and they wouldn't treat a man this way. But also, she was just a young girl, so homely and harmless. Just look at her.

# 27

At 3:23 on October 15, she woke with shooting pain in her stomach, stumbled to the bathroom, and turned on the light, exposing a trail of blood. At the sound of her scream he bolted upright in bed, wrapped her in a blanket, carried her to the car, and raced to the emergency room. They both knew.

\* \* \*

"The important thing is that you're all right," he said.

"You don't understand," she said, pushing him away.

"What?"

"I'm not all right. I lost the baby."

Don tried to take her hand, saying, "I know it's sad, it's hard. But I just mean that physically you're all right, and we'll try again."

Lorna leaned back, saying, "But that's the thing. We didn't try. We weren't planning. It just happened. That was my little miracle baby."

Don's shoulders drooped as he said, "I know, Lorna. It made me very happy. I wouldn't have thought that the idea of having a child would appeal to me at my age, but it did."

"This just changes everything, Don."

"What? Why?"

"I don't know."

Lorna wanted privacy, but at Mackey's urging, she did more interviews. Cindy Williams from CNN wanted to know how Lorna was feeling.

"Lorna, I am so sorry to hear about your miscarriage. I mention it only because my producers tell me that you are willing to talk about it."

"Thank you, Cindy. I'm not the first woman to miscarry, but that doesn't make it any easier. That wasn't *a* baby I lost. It was *my* baby. I loved my baby. I had hopes and plans."

"But are *you* OK, Lorna?"

"No, I don't think I'll ever be the same again. I can still have children. People tell me that's the main thing. And maybe that will matter to me at some point, but it doesn't matter to me now."

"Well, Lorna, you're brave to speak about this. I'm sure there are a lot of women watching who know exactly how you feel."

"That's just it, Cindy. I don't think there's anyone who knows *exactly* how I feel. But I suppose you're right that there are a lot of women who have lost babies and have had their own unique experiences of loss."

"This must be particularly difficult for you at this time, as you've become something of a national figure and your friend Sarah Andersen has been imprisoned."

"Yes, I wish Sarah had been there when I lost the baby. She would have known what to say and what not to say."

"So, she's on your mind?"

"Of course. Sarah has that innocent quality. There are some people who are troublemakers, people you can see being locked up. Sarah isn't one of them. I worry about her constantly."

"Do you think the worry, the stress, led to the miscarriage?"

"I know it did. It brought on a storm of emotions. I blame myself. I blame Sarah. But that's not right. We're not at fault. We're not to blame."

"Who is?"

"The military. They imprisoned Sarah. They set this chain in motion."

The *National Enquirer* headline the next day screamed "The Military Killed My Baby." It was absurd of course. The miscarriage probably just resulted from the body rejecting an unhealthy pregnancy, and even if the stress contributed to the miscarriage, it was a stretch to blame the military. But she had done it. Lorna had painted the military as not only wrongfully detaining poor, innocent Sarah but of killing a baby in the process.

It was a no-win situation for the military. If they released Sarah they would look like they were giving in to the hysterics of a manipulative woman, but if they kept Sarah detained they would look heartless. They chose to look heartless. The official response was silence, no comment, no statement.

The protesting crowd loved it. Batting-helmet boy had his bullhorn in the rain screaming about how the military killed Lorna's baby. That was one of the odd things about it. Plenty of pro-choice people lined up with Lorna, people who would never regard a fetus as a baby. It seemed to be enough for them in this case that Lorna regarded it as a baby. She intended to carry it to term, and so that made it a baby. "It's like throwing a pregnant woman down a flight of stairs," one of them said. "That's a crime. It's an assault on the woman, and it's manslaughter for the death of the child. Those military leaders need to be charged with the crime."

Lorna was self-conscious in watching and reading the reports and discussions. She had always been pro-choice herself, at least since leaving Virginia. In fact, she had planned on aborting the pregnancy at one point. If Don hadn't asked her to marry him that is what she would have done. When she decided to go through with the pregnancy, though, the baby had become real. It didn't make sense logically that her decision could change the mass of cells developing in her uterus from something insignificant into a person, but that is what had happened—she was sure of it.

Sarah was not allowed to communicate with the outside world, but she documented her detainment in a diary. The days were long with inactivity and dull with lack of news. She could only hope that Lorna was speaking out and getting attention, as they had planned. Then the guards told her about Lorna's miscarriage. Obviously, that had not been part of the plan, and Sarah assumed that had stopped Lorna. Now it was over for both of them. Sarah would linger in detainment awaiting court martial, and Lorna would lose the fight for secession.

But Sarah was wrong. Lorna kept the train rolling, and public sentiment was shifting. People had a right to choose, that was a fundamental American belief. FND had chosen to leave the Union. Of course their method was not ideal. It would have been better if they had settled on some little island off the coast of the United States and declared independence. Moving to North Dakota and outnumbering the native population was extreme and hostile, but sending in the military to vote was equally extreme and hostile. What was worse about it, though, was that it presumed to use the right to vote as a military weapon. It presumed to command soldiers in the one place where they surely could not be commanded, the voting booth. So Lorna started getting explicit. In another interview with Cindy Williams she said, "I'm calling on members of the military to vote their conscience. Don't give in to the pressure to vote against FND if you're not really against FND. And even if you are against FND, ask yourself whether you should be using your vote to oppose us. No one can make you vote."

"So, Lorna, are you suggesting that military personnel should refuse to go the polls?"

"No, Cindy. That's too dangerous. We've seen what happened to Sarah Andersen. I wouldn't ask any other member of the military to put themselves at risk the way Sarah did. All I'm suggesting is that people can ignore the referendum when they enter the voting booth. They can vote on other items and skip the referendum if they want."

"And no one has to know, right?"

"Right, no one has to know, Cindy. The soldiers will have done their duty as far as it can be compelled."

"But someone might say, 'Who is Lorna Kristman to be making these kinds of demands of the military?'"

"It's not a demand, Cindy. It's a suggestion. And it wasn't my idea. It was Sarah's. She told me about it during our last meeting at the diner, and if she hadn't been detained she would have been publicly urging her peers to go to the voting booth but skip the vote."

Sarah's husband Ben confirmed that Sarah had indeed devised this strategy, and "skip the vote" became the chant *du jour* among the protesters in Brooklyn, Seattle, and San Francisco.

There was no way to tell for sure how much impact the "skip the vote" mantra was having on the military, but support among the general public was climbing. In some national polls, as many as 52% of the general public said that they would either vote for secession or skip the referendum if they had the opportunity. The question was how that translated among the people who really counted, the military stationed in North Dakota. Most pundits speculated that support among this group was much lower.

# 28

"You just don't get it, Don."

"OK."

"Don't OK me."

Don turned to face her on the couch. "All right. What don't I get?"

"What it's like to be used."

"Who's using you?

"Everyone."

Don squinted. "Who?"

Lorna shook her open hands at him. "The media, FND, Mackey, you. Everyone is using me."

Don slumped back on the couch. "Lorna, the media sure. But you're using them back. It's a two-way street. But FND? Mackey? Me? We all appreciate what you're doing. Deeply. And you're running the show. You're in charge."

"I'm tired of it."

"Tired of what?"

"Tired of pretending I'm in charge. I was never in charge. The john is always the one in charge."

"You're right, Lorna, but that life is behind you. Nobody is paying you now."

Lorna leaned in, poking her finger at him. "That's a distinction without a difference, Don."

"A what?"

"I've been talking to Casey. And she says…"

"To who?"

"Casey. Your old girlfriend. She says…"

"You've been in touch with her all this time?"

"No, Don. But she's been in North Dakota all this time, since she left New York."

"What is she doing?"

"She's a dominatrix, and she says they're using me."

"She's a what?"

"I'm just the face and, I guess, the hot body of all this. FND is not my movement. It's Mackey's, maybe it's yours. And sure, there are half a million other people here who believed in it enough to move to fuckin' North Dakota. But my heart's not in it anymore. I've been doing it to please you, to give myself a sense of purpose. But when I lost that baby I lost all sense of purpose."

"Lorna, it's understandable. Your body, your hormones, everything...since the baby..."

Lorna turned purple. "Don't talk to me about hormones, Don. You have no fuckin' idea. You've never felt like this."

"You're right, I'm sure I haven't. So what do you want to do? What can I do for you?"

"I want out."

"Out of what?"

"FND, the whole thing."

"But, Lorna, the referendum is in a couple of weeks. What about Sarah?"

"Sarah is the only thing that keeps me going at this point."

"All right, Lorna. Let me talk to Mackey."

Did Lorna want out of their relationship too? There had been no talk of a wedding since the miscarriage. He realized that she was a storm of emotions and that the past was eating at her in a way it hadn't before. Some lines you cross and you don't come back. Lorna had always insisted on referring to herself as a whore even though she hadn't worked as a prostitute for years. She hadn't been coerced into prostitution; she had made the decision of her own free will. If anyone could have been unharmed by that life it was Lorna. But who goes through life unharmed?

Don hadn't been to the diner in months, but he called Mackey and told him he was coming with something serious to discuss.

Sitting at a booth in the back, he said, "Lorna wants out."

"What do you mean?" Mackey asked.

"She wants out of making speeches and doing media. She feels like she's being used."

"Well yeah, the media are using her, but we're using the media right back."

"That's not her point, Mack. She feels like FND is using her, that this isn't really her fight, her cause, that she's just been doing it to please me or to please people in general."

"That's not true, Don. She's a true believer. I've heard her speaking with people one on one."

"I know. But she's had all these feelings come up since the miscarriage. Maybe it's hormonal. But she's been reconsidering her whole life. You know the way she always referred to herself as a whore? I always took that as her way of owning her identity, of feeling no shame. Maybe that's what she was trying to do, but I'm not sure it ever worked. It's definitely not working now. She's feeling like she's always been manipulated."

Mackey wiped his brow. "Shit, but she can't just withdraw now. We're almost there. What will we tell people?"

"I don't know, Mack. But that's what she wants to do. The only reason she's continued to this point is that she feels responsible for Sarah."

"Let me talk to Summers and see what he suggests."

The next day Mackey phoned Don and asked, "Can you get her to give one last speech for Sarah?"

"I think so."

"Good. Summers says that after that we can tell the media that Lorna is ill and under doctor's orders to rest."

"Will people buy that?"

"They'll have to. It's the best we can do."

Don brought the idea back to Lorna, saying, "I talked to Mackey.

He's sorry that you're feeling used the way you are. He didn't ever mean to use you."

"Oh, fuck him. He's a master manipulator."

"Well, he doesn't want you to do anything that you don't want to do."

"How kind."

"Would you be willing to give one more speech for Sarah demanding her release? Mackey talked to Summers, and his idea is that if you did that then we could say afterwards that you're ill and under doctor's orders to rest."

"But who would buy that bullshit?"

"I don't know, Lorna. That's just the best we could come up with. Will you do it?"

"I'll do it for Sarah. I used her the way people used me. I owe it to her."

"Thank you, Lorna. I'll tell Mackey and have him set up the time and place."

# 29

Charlie Foreman was drilling his militia at the compound when he got the call from Glen Summers.

"We're going to have to go with the emergency plan."

"Just say where and when, Glen."

"That's being decided and arranged. I'll let you know. You still have your man inside?"

"Deep in."

"No connections?"

"He's red, white, and blue all the way."

"I'll arrange the financials."

# 30

"On your knees, wimp."

Glen Summers stood still and raped her with his eyes.

"I said on your knees, wimp."

"You went too far, Casey. Everyone likes a good game of spank and tickle. Hell, I even enjoyed the blackmail up to a point. But when you talked to Lorna you crossed the line."

"I said on your knees, wimp."

He pointed a revolver at her head.

"Game's over, Casey."

\* \* \*

Don turned his pillow over again and tried to clear his mind. The thoughts returned like roaches. Lorna was going. She hadn't said it. She didn't have to. She might stick around until after the referendum, but not a day longer. Where would she go? Somewhere warm. Mexico? Florida? California? She needed to be warm. So did he. What a fool he had been, falling in love with a prostitute and chasing secession movements. So what would he do? Go back to New York and reconnect with his daughter, get to know the grandkids again? Yeah, probably, but would that fill the hole in him?

He would have to start writing again, not these blogs that got him into all this. Fiction, that's where his escape was, and that's what he needed—to create a new world with new people in it. Lorna might say that sounded like more of a need to control, but that wasn't quite right. You didn't really get to control those people, your characters. They surprised you; they did things you didn't expect. You could plan out adventures for them, but they went down roads you didn't have in mind, even took you to endings you didn't foresee. Publishing fiction again would mean lining the pockets of his ex-wife, but it would be worth it. Of course, he could decide just to write for himself and not publish any of it, but that wouldn't be satisfying. The idea of an audience was essential. It kept you honest, made you edit and revise your work. Besides, Don needed to connect with people who would care about the characters he created. He mixed some Metamucil and decided to push.

Summers arranged for Lorna to speak at the university in Fargo. It had not been announced that this would be Lorna's final speech, nor was she supposed to allude to that fact. So she drew a crowd and some media, but nothing extraordinary. As a group, the students at North Dakota State were not friendly to FND; their tuition would triple without taxpayers' supplements after secession. Still, there were some students ideologically committed to the movement and, of course, enamored of Lorna. The police presence was heavy, as it had usually been at such events. But it was the military presence that really bothered people, even those opposing FND. It just seemed so heavy-handed and unnecessary. They were there to keep the peace, but they seemed more likely to cause trouble than prevent it.

Lorna's speech was stock and uninspired, as she thanked her hosts and paid tribute to the university as an incubator of free thought and new ideas. Her tone shifted, though, becoming impassioned and angry when she spoke of Sarah.

"Ideas are dangerous and messy, especially if you believe in them, especially if you act on them. Sarah Andersen can tell you that. Oh wait, no, she can't, because she's not allowed to speak. Sarah has been detained in an undisclosed location, supposedly in North Dakota, but who knows where she really is? Not her husband, Ben. He hasn't been allowed to speak with her in weeks. I guess we're just supposed to trust the government and trust the military that they're taking good care of Sarah wherever she is."

Lorna felt good. She was hitting her stride with the speech, and she thought to herself that maybe she had been making too much of things. Maybe she would patch things up with Don and see this through to the end. She continued, "Obviously Sarah needs to be locked up. A woman who would disobey a direct order and visit a diner to talk about secession is nothing but trouble. Come on! If Sarah's plight doesn't highlight the tyranny that we have been living under in the United States, I don't know what does. Free people must be allowed to think freely and make free decisions. It's time to let her go."

Lorna paused for a small group to echo "let her go," but their chant was broken by a bang. Lorna hit the ground. The crowd screamed and dispersed, ushered through the exits of the auditorium. The police and military surrounded the shooter.

# 31

It didn't register, couldn't be real. Don's stomach knew it, but his head couldn't process the news. He had just been with her this morning. She was almost out, just about safe, going to California or wherever. Only one more speech.

No one had taped the shooter in the act, but there was video of Lorna being blown back and then disappearing from view as she hit the ground behind the podium. There had been just one shot, but it found its target, striking Lorna in the head. Security and police stormed the stage. An ambulance arrived minutes later.

The national news media interrupted programming to report the story, "Lorna Kristman has been shot by an unidentified gunman while giving a speech at North Dakota State University." The identity of the gunman was not a matter of dispute for the police and military, but for the moment they refused to confirm the identity for the press, saying only that a suspect had been taken into custody for questioning. Immediately, though, the rumors began to fly that the shooter was a member of the military. Students in attendance posted to Facebook and Twitter about it, and they spoke to reporters who arrived on the scene. Still, by that evening the military and the police would say only that a suspect had been taken into custody.

Lorna's condition was described as critical. Don had difficulty getting to see her. No, he was not her husband. They lived together, they were engaged, sort of. She had no family in North Dakota. Yes, he was her emergency contact person.

The shooter, Corporal Lance Widner, announced his own responsibility through a timed post to a blog, a pre-recorded video of him making the following statement: "This afternoon I shot the traitor, Lorna Kristman. I took this action in the service of my country and with the support of my superiors. This will be denied. The truth will be suppressed, but I assure you I was not acting alone. I can also assure you that I am of sound mind. On this site I have posted my official military psychological evaluation as well as an independent evaluation by a civilian psychiatrist. I realize that my action will be judged to be a crime. Because of my love for the United States of America I am willing to pay the price. I did not make this decision or take this action in haste. It was the only way to stop the secession. I am confident that history will judge me a hero even if a court judges me otherwise."

The blog was shut down quickly, but not before the video and the files could be copied and spread all around the internet. The Army replied with a statement saying that Corporal Widner had confessed to the shooting and that despite his video statement he had acted alone. There were no orders or support from superior officers.

Lorna had been taken into surgery, but there was nothing the doctors could do. As the most graphic videos from the scene had shown, the bullet had splattered her brain on the stage. She was pronounced dead at 3:16 p.m. on October 25.

The news spread and the protests flared with renewed chants of "let her go." But who did they want let go? Lorna was gone. Sarah? North Dakota? News reporters summarized Lorna's rapid rise to national fame, and FND members gave interviews paying tribute to Lorna.

Don was silent, avoiding requests for interviews. He wished he had been at the speech. Rationally, he knew he couldn't have done anything, but he still had a sense that it would have made a difference. Lorna didn't want him there, though. He arranged for a small private funeral. Lorna's family in Virginia did not accept his invitation to attend, nor did they want to see to the remains. Lorna was cremated. Don planned to scatter her ashes someplace warm.

The blogosphere exploded with discussion and debate concerning Corporal Lance Widner. Had he acted alone? Or had he actually been following orders that his superiors could not give officially? Was he insane? Widner's family and friends in Lisbon, Ohio spoke of a young man who loved his country and had wanted to serve in the Army since he was a boy. Growing up post 9/11, he had idolized soldiers. They had always been his heroes. There were no warning signs that he was unstable or that he had a plan to kill Lorna Kristman. No one could believe that he had done it.

# 32

Snow blanketed much of North Dakota for the final week of October. Tempers flared across the country, but North Dakota was cold, sunny, and quiet, waiting for the referendum. Pundits speculated about how Lorna's death—sometimes they said "murder" and sometimes "assassination," but mostly they said "death"—would affect the vote. Surely, if Widner's intention was to stop FND at the ballot box his plan was ill-conceived. Lorna's death had greatly increased support for FND nationally.

Sarah Andersen remained in military detention. The brass and the administration decided it would be a sign of weakness to give in to mob demands for her release.

The sun shone brightly over the North Dakota prairie on the first Tuesday in November. People lined up outside the polling stations before they opened, and lines kept people waiting for hours in many places. Special polling booths were set up at the military camps. By the end of the day over a million voters had gone to the polls but fewer than a million had actually voted on the referendum. Apparently half the military had abstained. The referendum passed. North Dakota would secede from the United States.

# 33

Charlie Foreman and Glen Summers met for a drink in a roadhouse bar outside Owl, North Dakota.

"We won."

"Sometimes you have to get your hands dirty."

Foreman nodded.

"But what if Widner breaks?" Summers asked.

"He won't have time to. He'll be committing suicide later today."

"The money?" asked Foreman.

"Wired to an account in the Caymans so that his family can claim it."

"But they won't, right?"

"Of course not. We'll wire it back. No trace."

Yes, that's how Don imagined it as he sat on the toilet. Maybe it was true. Who knew? Don could feel it coming. He was about to write again. He had always known that no story was purely fictional. Every story was inspired by something real and someone real. Now he had learned a corollary: No story was ever purely true. No one knew the full truth, and they would not be able to tell it true even if they did. That was OK because there could still be a truth in fiction, even a truth in lies. You just had to know how to arrange the *Tetris* pieces. His new book would be something different. Don grabbed the pen and paper that he kept near the toilet. He cleared his mind, gave a push, and began to write the story of Free Dakota.

# Acknowledgments

This book would never have been written without the love and support of my wife, Megan Lloyd. In addition to doing more than her fair share of just about everything at home, Megan was my first and best reader, providing invaluable feedback on multiple drafts of the novel. My friend Eric Bronson was also a tremendous support with comments on multiple drafts. Eric has a gift for combining just the right amount of encouragement and criticism. The support of Megan and Eric would have been more than I could have hoped for, but they were not alone in helping me. Friends and former students were kind enough to take an interest in what I was writing. Susie Addoms, Jess Baranousky, Trip Johnson, Ryan Klubeck, Abby Myers, Ashley Panko, and Mike Pasquini all read and commented on various drafts. The book is better because of them. No doubt I have absentmindedly neglected to include some names. If yours is one of them, please forgive me. Finally, I must thank Laurie Smith, who provided the perfect photograph for the cover. I haven't seen the wild horses of North Dakota with my own eyes, but Laurie's stunning photograph captures them as I have imagined them in all their majestic beauty.

# About the Author

William Irwin is Herve A. LeBlanc Distinguished Service Professor and Chair of Philosophy at King's College (Pennsylvania) and is the author of *The Free Market Existentialist: Capitalism without Consumerism*. He is also the author of *Intentionalist Interpretation: A Philosophical Explanation and Defense*. Irwin originated the philosophy and popular culture genre of books with *Seinfeld and Philosophy* (1999), *The Simpsons and Philosophy* (2001), and *The Matrix and Philosophy* (2002). *Free Dakota* is his first novel. He would love to hear from readers through e-mail at williamirwin@kings.edu.

At Roundfire we publish great stories. We lean towards the spiritual and thought-provoking. But whether it's literary or popular, a gentle tale or a pulsating thriller, the connecting theme in all Roundfire fiction titles is that once you pick them up you won't want to put them down.